CLAWS AND STARSHIPS

CLAWS AND STARSHIPS
A PELTED SHORT STORY COLLECTION

M. C. A. HOGARTH

Claws and Starships
A Pelted Short Story Collection
First edition, copyright 2011 by M.C.A. Hogarth

M. Hogarth
PMB 109
4522 West Village Dr.
Tampa, FL 33624

ISBN-13: 978-1490427225
ISBN-10: 1490427228

Cover art by MCA Hogarth

Designed & typeset by Catspaw DTP Services
http://www.catspawdtp.com/

TABLE OF CONTENTS

A Distant Sun

ELLEN PROPPED A FOOT on the arm of a dark green chair and glanced at his teenaged students, seated in various levels of discomfort on the sofas, chairs and ottomans. He loved the first day of class, and the first day of this one in particular. The teacher pointed to a sturdily-built gray Hinichi wolfine: mostly human, with a fine covering of wolf.

"You, my friend. What's your name?"

"Uh, Derrick, sir. Derrick Lombard."

"Very good," Kellen said, "Tell me what class this is?"

Bewildered, the wolfine's eyes sought the others', hoping for support. "Err, it's 'Ethical Perspectives on History', sir."

Kellen grinned. "Ah! Thank you, Derrick. That's just what I wanted to hear." An uneasy chuckle rose from the others watching, and he folded his arms across his chest. "As you might have guessed, I'm new here. My name is Kellen Grove. I ask that you call me 'Mr. Grove' so we can at least pretend you respect me, but otherwise my rules are as informal as my classroom. I like a lively discussion, so make free with your comments, particularly your jokes. I expect you to answer my questions; in return, I'll answer yours, no matter how hard. Make no mistake: there will be hard questions. This will be far and away the most difficult and interesting elective being offered during your last year of high school, and I'm gratified that you have all chosen to take it."

"History is the most difficult topic we're going to have all year?" a slim black human asked in an arch contralto.

Kellen laughed, his dark ears flipping forward. "What's your name?"

"Rachel Myers, sir!"

He slid off the chair. "Stand up, please, Rachel. I prefer to illustrate my answers concretely. You! The russet Aera there. Name?"

"Madeira, Clan Flait," was the wary reply from the slender girl more vulpine than humanoid.

"Stand up for me, please, Madeira. You? Donegan Unfound? Yes, thank you, just like that. You?" he turned to an ivory Karaka'An feline, her thin legs folded beneath her on the vast dark blue chair. Kellen faltered as he stared at her eyes. They were green? No, only one of them. The other was a yellowish lime color just similar enough to force the viewer to look twice.

"Margeaux Davis," she said in a shy soprano, lifting her odd-colored eyes to meet his.

"Ah, yes, stand for me, please, Margeaux."

Delivering himself a mental shake, he picked out two more students, then folded his arms across his chest again, tossing his black jaw ruffs behind his shoulders.

"Now," Kellen said. "Someone tell me what all these people have in common."

He watched with concealed amusement as they exchanged looks in none-too-covert bafflement. One of the braver ones managed to speak.

"In common, sir? I guess, they're all here?"

Kellen laughed. "That's a good start, but we're in History, not Physics. Any other ideas?"

"They're all two-footed," someone suggested from the back.

"Good!" Kellen said, fox-like ears perking. "Give me more on that track."

"They all have hands," said a male Phoenix, his own wings twitching.

The female human beside him added, "And they're all bilaterally symmetrical!"

A low rustle ran through the classroom as its members stared at the girl.

Kellen grinned. "Budding biologist, eh? She's right, though. These are all good observations, but you're citing the effects of a single root cause. Can you guess what it is?" He waited through the ensuing silence, then stood and walked behind Rachel, the black human. "How about 99% of their genome?"

"I thought this was History, not Biology," another human said, a lopsided smile on his face.

"It is History," Kellen said, finger snaking out to point at him. "Do you know your own? How the Alliance formed? Who formed it . . . and how they evolved?"

"We didn't evolve," a pantherine said. "Everyone knows that. The humans made us centuries ago."

"Precisely," said Kellen, resting against one of the taller chairs. "And the primary things that will engage us this year are the implications, complications and consequences of that decision. An ethical perspective, if you will. You may sit, everyone. Thank you for your patience." He turned to Rachel and said, "Do you understand now what I mean by this class being your most difficult this year?"

"Uh, I'm not sure," she admitted. "What's so hard about figuring out the implications of the first gengineering?"

"Did you know that seventy percent of the individuals who left on the generation ships to colonize the original Core planets couldn't successfully conceive and bear young?" Kellen asked, waited for her to shake her head. The rest of the class was staring at him now. "Do you know why?" Another negative. "Fully sixty-five percent of them had been engineered as sex toys. Because of concern that they would accidentally cause 'complications' when used, most of them were created without generative organs."

Since grim silence had been his intention, Kellen was satisfied with their response. "These are details adults don't share with children, for good reason. The creation of another sapient life form is an event fraught with ethical dilemmas. The solutions originally proposed and implemented for the first gengineered creatures on Terra were not always the best ones, and examining them is often cause for thought . . . and nightmare. You are no longer children. It's time for you to examine our shared history: its atrocities and tragedies as well as the positive outcomes that have become our birthright. That is why this is a difficult class."

"I see," the human girl said, subdued.

"You will," Kellen promised.

A hearty slap against his shoulder-blade jerked Kellen from his reverie at the window.

"Hey!" A scarlet Tam-illee foxine with brilliant gold eyes steadied him, grinning. "Sorry 'bout that, *arii*." The word for "friend" jarred; Kellen wasn't used to hearing it. "It's quite a view, isn't it?"

"It is," Kellen murmured, glancing back at the waterfall running down the rocks. Silvergate Academy was nestled in the shallow face of a mountain, a virtue that had largely decided Kellen on the move. It was a far cry from the beaches and hardy, water-starved shrubs from which he'd come and he'd needed the change of scenery.

"My name's Joet Starsteps. I teach astronomy here. You'll be sharing a suite with me upstairs." The man grinned amiably. "It'll be nice to have company! Half the faculty live off the premises."

"I'm new to the city," Kellen said. "I thought it would be easier staying here until I got oriented."

"Ah, yes. I heard you were from out of town. They say you came highly recommended!"

Kellen smiled wryly. "So highly recommended I got fired."

Joet snorted. "Ah well. Some schools will do that for teaching things they wouldn't want their kids to know. Silvergate knows better. The administration's been hungering for years for someone who would dust history off and make it a little more palatable to teenagers. Would you like to see your room?"

"Very much," Kellen admitted. "It was a long day."

Joet nodded, waving a hand toward the corridor leading away from the glass wall. "I did wonder," he said. "You could have moved in today and started teaching tomorrow. . . ."

"There's too much material to cover to skip a day, particularly with the seniors," Kellen said, picking up the small bag at his feet. "It throws them off their stride to have a substitute the first day. Besides . . . first days are always fun."

"Iley Ever-laughing! You pack light. Don't tell me that's your only bag?" Joet shook his head. "Come on, there's a stairwell up the hall and to your right. So, how long have you been teaching?"

"Since a while after I got my second degree. Almost six years now."

"How old are you?

Kellen said, "Thirty-four by Alliance Mean."

Joet nodded. "I'm thirty-seven. Been teaching nine years, and five of them here. It's a god-blessedly good school."

"So I've heard," Kellen said. He padded into the stairwell, his own unshod paws quieter than Joet's booted feet. "Astronomy, ah? We should talk about our schedules. Maybe I can get some of the course work on the diaspora to match with your lectures on the Core worlds."

"You're a driven man, *arii*," Joet said, his chuckle sounding behind Kellen's shoulder. "I like that in a suite-mate."

They reached the top of the stairs, and the tall, scarlet foxine led Kellen to the end of the hall. A wall of glass like the one downstairs terminated the corridor, providing a view of the water cascading down the rocks, the roar muted by a force-field noticeable only by its two tiny transmitters at the ceiling and floor.

"Joet Starsteps," the foxine said to the ID panel, then grinned down at Kellen. "Here's home . . . after you."

Kellen lifted his bag for the last time and walked into the den, a modest room with a clay-gray carpet, half the size of one of the ground-floor classrooms. Its entire southern wall, a sheet of glass set into the mountain, shone with the diffuse light of a coppery sunset. The navy blue sofa against the back wall faced a coffee table. To the right, a long bar marked off the kitchenette, a row of three goldwood stools tucked beneath it. Aside from the wallscreen by the door, the window wall, and one hanging tapestry in bright gold and sienna brown, nothing broke the austerity of the room. Two doors framed the sofa.

"I'm in the one on the left," Joet said. "It has a window onto rock, but I like to count the colored striations when I can't sleep." He winked.

Kellen smiled, black ears swiveling forward, and stepped into his new room. Larger than his last, it held a goldwood bureau, a small night-table and a single-person bed. A full-length mirror and a closed door were the only other decorations. "What's this?" he asked, tapping the wooden door jamb with a knuckle.

"That's the bathroom."

"We're sharing a bathroom?" Kellen asked, the fur along his spine lifting.

Joet chuckled. "Yeah. So I hope you're a neat freak."

"As long as you don't use my grooming tools, we'll be fine," Kellen said, forcing a smile. "By the way, where do you requisition materials for your classroom? There are a couple of things I'd like to pick up."

"On the ground floor, on the opposite side of the building. It's across from the headmaster's office. It should still be open."

"I think I'll check. Thank you, Joet."

Joet waved and grinned. "You're welcome. I'll see you later . . . ?"

"Probably not," Kellen said. "The way I feel, I'll fall right to sleep when I get back."

Joet chuckled. "I've been there. Have a good evening, then."

Several hours later, Kellen jerked upright in his new bed, oil-sweat matting the fur on his back. He panted, staring at the wall, then touched his neck, his chest. So much thicker than sweat, but of course the scientists had to cross the genes up somewhere and give the fox-based creatures that would eventually become the Seersa a strange oil-sweat combination that did the job of neither very well.

He rubbed his fingers over his forehead, then glanced at the mirror across from the bed: black body, with only the striking white splash across chest, neck, arms, and the bottom of his mouth floating, pale against the dark.

He slid out of bed and padded cautiously to the bathroom, peering inside to ensure its lack of occupancy. A wave of his hand and the tap flared on, spouting a writhing thread of water.

Kellen combed his jaw ruffs with cold, wet fingers, then drew his thumb across the bridge of his nose and dry lips. He tilted his head back and sighed, summoning the images from the nightmare: the usual parade of sticky ropes, obscenely corded like skinned flesh, composed of oily red and viscous white fluid, pulling around him, choking him. He stared at the ceiling and composed himself. The nightmare had not come as a surprise. He only hoped that he could unexpectedly fall back to sleep.

"Do you need help with that?" a soft soprano asked behind him.

Kellen glanced over his shoulder wearily, using the wall to steady his precarious perch on the stool. The mirror the supply office had given him hung between his white hands. "I . . . think I'll be fine." He squinted, trying to place the ivory Karaka'An feline with the delicate limbs. "Margeaux, isn't it? Shouldn't you be home?"

"I signed up for afterschool," she said, smiling.

"Oh!" Kellen sealed the mirror to the strip, then leaned back. "Is that straight?"

The girl stepped away and cocked her head, lank honey-pale hair sliding over one ear. "Yes."

"So what's afterschool?" he asked, climbing off the stool. He glanced up in time to see her odd-colored eyes widen; whipping around, Kellen flung his hands onto the mirror as it slid toward the floor a few seconds before Margeaux's slender hand grasped its edge.

With the mirror steady beneath the pressure of his hands, Kellen let out a sigh, eyes drifting toward the thin, small fingers: almost too thin. They looked like a baby's beside his.

"You have large hands," the girl said, wonderingly. "A musician's hands. Do you play?"

"I . . . no." Kellen grimaced, tail tightly curled. He pushed the mirror up, sealed it properly and turned his back to it. "So . . . afterschool?"

Margeaux stepped back. "It counts toward your extracurricular points. You sign up to stay after school with a teacher, help him plan lessons or clean up or whatever he needs."

Kellen paused, ears flicking sideways. "That's a good idea," he murmured. "We didn't have that at Barry." He picked up the stool and paused, realizing that the girl was still there, tail curled around her dainty ankles. "Ah . . . let me guess. History fascinates you and you want to be my apprentice."

"Yes," she answered.

Kellen stopped. He'd been joking. "Really?"

"Unless you'd rather not?" Margeaux shifted her weight from one foot to the other. He watched the sway of her hips, mind wandering with fatigue to an assessment inspired by the sight: she had an Attenuated Body Frame A, definitely. Seventy percent more prone to posture and bone problems than the Stockier Nominal Body Frame A like his own.

Reining in his thoughts, Kellen said, "Of course

you're welcome. I'm sorry. I'm a little slow today."

"You look tired," Margeaux said, a smile parting her lips. Her gentle and oddly intent bicolored gaze settled on him. "Can I help unpack?"

"There are some blankets and ornaments in those," said Kellen, indicating the row of boxes nearest the door. "You can arrange them around the room."

The girl crouched beside the first and pulled its flap open. She dragged out a thick scarlet afghan. "Mr. Grove, were you always this informal about teaching?"

"Probably," Kellen answered. "Honestly, it's been so long since I started. . . ." He trailed off, then chuckled and sat on one of the large, cushioned chairs. Propping his heavy, animal-jointed feet on the center table, he spread tomorrow's lesson plans on his data tablet and suppressed a yawn. "I've always believed talking to a person is more effective than talking at them."

A soft wheeze caught Kellen's attention. He glanced at her: she was smothering a giggle. His dark brows lifted.

"I'm sorry. I wish I'd had more teachers like that. My first school was nothing like Silvergate." The girl folded her long legs to one side and lifted a glazed bowl. "The nicest teacher there was Mrs. Skyeyes. She taught us history, but it was specific to events after the Founding." Her eyes flicked to his face. "She never told us about the roots of things."

"You were probably young," said Kellen, letting his eyes close for just a moment. "As I said yesterday, these are not topics for children."

The cinnamon scent of fresh kerinne roused him, blinking a crust of sleep from his eyes. The afghan draped over the seat had migrated onto his lap. Familiar, carefully collected bowls and paintings adorned the tables and walls, and a large rug dominated the floor with its aggressive palette of earth browns, bright reds and mineral yellows.

"Don't you sleep at night?" Margeaux asked, holding one of the only items he hadn't seen in his cursory sweep of the room, a brass figurine of a twisted, writhing body.

"Occasionally," he said, chagrined. "How long was I unconscious, doctor? Is it terminal?"

She bleated her soft, smothered laugh and said, "Only half an hour." The slim girl shifted uncomfortably, then held out the figurine. "Mr. Grove, what is this?"

The Seersa didn't have to look at it. He'd memorized it long ago with fingertips and eyes. "Jazeen's 'Mortal Coil'."

"It's beautiful," she said in a low, uncertain voice.

Kellen glanced at her sharply. She balanced the figurine's heavy base against her fragile ribcage and cradled it in both hands, studying it with a face so gentle it almost obscured the horror and fascination written across brows and ears and mouth. She lifted her bicolored gaze to his, self-consciousness abruptly crimping her shoulders, and then ducked her head.

"It is," the girl said again, defiant. She walked to the middle of the circle of chairs and throw-pillows and set it on the table's naked center.

Again that night, Kellen woke gasping, a pillow crushed in his hands. His sodden sheets clung to him and he lurched away, unable to stand their clammy touch. Bodies this time, strangled in ropes, clutching the sky, all helplessly, youthfully female. Angry, he stripped the bed sheets and dumped them in the laundry chute before entering the bathroom. A soft command activated the shower head and a night light. Kellen slipped under the hot water, baring his teeth.

He'd bought 'Mortal Coil' over twelve years ago, motivated by an ambivalence with roots in hatred and need. It had always been displayed in his classroom, but on a tall shelf, far from careless hands and unfocused eyes. To see it affect someone else as it had obviously been meant to. . . .

Kellen sighed, running his fingers through his short head-hair as water slicked his fur to his body. He concentrated on the steam funneled through his demi-muzzle's long nose, the faint odor of the disinfectant soap he favored, the rough tiles beneath the pads on his broad, dish-like feet. When the water ran out, he used a towel instead of the air-dryer to keep from waking Joet.

His ablutions cleaned his thoughts along with his body. Breathing easier, Kellen threw on a robe and padded to the kitchen. The kerinne Margeaux had concocted earlier sounded good. Brewing it the time-consuming way with ground cinnamon and milk in a pot soothed him. He poured the result into a mug and turned to the couch.

"Do you always wake up an hour before dawn?" Joet asked, his voice a hoarse croak.

Kellen jumped back, almost splashing himself. "Joet! I'm sorry, I didn't hear you. . . ."

The taller Tam-illee yawned, his face screwing into a fearful grimace. He tottered into the kitchen and said, "No worries. I couldn't sleep . . ." He paused again to yawn, "but Iley be blessed if I'm not still tired." He peered at Kellen blearily. "You don't look so well yourself."

"Ah, well. Sleeping in a new bed . . . I need time to adjust." Kellen took his mug to the couch, ears splayed.

Joet rummaged in one of the cabinets. "You sure?" he asked again, his voice clearing. "You look a little peaked."

Kellen studied the reflection of stars broken by the falling water. "There are parts of history that keep me up at night," he said, deciding on a piece of the truth. "If you ever grow comfortable with them, you do your students a disservice."

Joet leaned over the counter, hands clasping an empty mug. "There's something to be said for a little academic distance, if only to keep up one's physical health."

The Seersa smiled without humor. "I'd rather be too close to a subject than too far from it."

Joet issued no reply for several minutes, prompting Kellen to look that way. The Tam-illee foxine's gold eyes rested on him, curious, considering. Slowly, Kellen rotated his black ears forward.

The Tam-illee smiled. "You know, Kellen, Silvergate has a reputation for turning out lots of tech people. Engineers, scientists, doctors, that sort. The artists, poets and historians are harder to find . . . probably because they're harder to teach."

Kellen pressed his hands around the walls of his mug. "Artists don't need teaching. They need inspiring."

Joet grinned. "Is that so."

Kellen glanced at him with a crooked smile. "You know. Just an opinion from a soft sciences type."

"Riiiight," Joet said, still grinning. He shook his head and poured himself some coffee. "I'm for a shower and an early start, I guess. I might even catch a few stars left on the horizon when I get out. Enjoy your breakfast, *arii*."

The smaller man smiled. "Thanks."

"Mr. Grove."

Kellen set aside his data tablet and stood, his fingers resting on the edge of the hard-backed chair. "Headmaster. Good morning."

Headmaster Irina Darteriov of Silvergate refused to be called 'headmistress', and no one dared disagree. Black slacks and an ultramarine blouse should have accentuated the length of the Harat-Shar cheetaine's limbs, but the direct, focused orange eyes and black stripes framing her nose and mouth unfailingly pulled the viewer back to her austere face.

Darteriov tapped the data tablet she'd brought against her wrist. "I hope you're finding things satisfactory here at Silvergate, Mr. Grove."

Kellen managed a lopsided grin. "The week I've been here has been pleasant, Headmaster."

"Good." She flashed the data tablet at him. "Perhaps you can explain this extravagant requisition? We're a smaller school than your last. We don't have money to toss to the sands."

The Seersa cleared his throat. "The science departments all have amphitheater-style immersive 3deo viewers. I'm only asking for a projection model."

"The science departments have justified their need for such expenses," said Darteriov. "What would you use such an installation for?"

Kellen's tail flicked once. "To begin, I'd like to broadcast the Touchground festivals on Tam-ley next month. And then there's the archeology summit on Karaka'Ana, and the university-sponsored debate on the artificial creation of the Core languages just after the diaspora, and the gengineered complications conference. . . ."

The headmaster waved her hand, the data tablet sparkling in the early sunlight. "Enough. Write it down and have it ready for me tomorrow."

He met her gaze, determination stretching his mouth into a tight line. "I can have it by the end of today."

"Then do so." She slipped the tablet under an arm and strode out.

"All right . . . throw, Richard!"

The class watched with avid interest as the human planted his feet then casually tossed the dart. It struck the flickering board, pegging a vivid red light that flashed twice before settling on a steady glow.

"Sorry!" Kellen said, "I'm afraid you died in vitro from complications."

Rachel, the human girl, rasped an aggravated sound. "No one lived!"

The dark Seersa leaned against one of the chairs. "Is that true? Did anyone make it past the in vitro stage?"

Margeaux and the Phoenix, Cyclone, waved their

hands.

"Once each, right?"

They murmured assent, and Kellen lifted two fingers above his head. "That's two. Two out of how many throws? Twenty each, so that's two hundred? Two out of two hundred. Not very good odds, is it."

"What kind of game were those iddlewits playing?" Rachel demanded, crossing her arms. "If this is right, they killed hundreds of babies! It's sick, Mr. Grove!"

"It was just a procedure," Richard said, plucking his dart off the electronic board. Two weeks of classes had acclimated the seniors to the informality of Kellen's teaching, and the human demonstrated their comfort by addressing Rachel directly. "They had to do it over and over to get it right, like they would any other scientific experiment. Would you rather they would have let the things live when they would have been born crippled?"

"And who would have taken care of them?" Margeaux asked, fingers touching her lower lip. She sat on one of the oversized sofa-chairs, her thin limbs tucked gracefully beneath her.

"That's a valid point," Kellen said. "The corporations in charge of this project didn't have the overhead to set up care facilities for their rejects. Or would you have wanted to take care of something so mangled it barely looked alive and couldn't breathe without a machine?"

The students shifted, uncomfortable.

Rachel said, "Still, it's hardly fair. Hardly . . . moral."

Kellen's black brow arched. "Is it?" he asked pointedly.

The students erupted into wild discussion. Kellen listened to as many threads as he could, ears flicking, and measured the passion in the room. He smiled as he lifted his hands.

"Enough! I hear two definite opinions. One is that it's kinder to kill something before it's born than to let it live a short and miserable life. The other is that to kill something you made before it's born, for whatever reason, is immoral, and that you should take responsibility for your actions . . . that any kind of life, no matter how short or difficult, has the potential for meaning. Is that a reasonable summary?" At their nods, he continued, "So is it safe to say that there are two separate issues to consider, that of the victim's life and that of the responsibility of the creator?"

The class murmured their agreement. Kellen picked up a dart and tossed it at the board, scoring himself a vibrant green light—healthy body, retarded mind. "The game of life is risky enough without your chances being depressed by serving as the test subject for a new scientific process. Tonight, I want you to write three essays for case studies on the two possible outcomes: a life destroyed before its birth and a life allowed to live no matter the complications. Do each point of view: the scientist and the test subject. Then tomorrow, I'll tell you a real story of one man's solution to this particular problem."

Rachel paused, then said, "Uh, Mr. Grove? Just three essays?"

Kellen smiled, eyes dark. "So you caught that, did you, Rachel? You won't have to write an essay for the subject who wasn't allowed to live. But you should probably consider it, don't you think?"

Kellen dropped onto a chair and let his head fall back against the cushions. His hand absently caressed the knobby fabric on the chair's arm as he reviewed the lesson plan for the following day, wondering just where the past three weeks had flown.

"I'm sure you didn't look this tired the first week," Margeaux said, the aroma of hot cocoa accompanying her. Kellen opened his eyes quickly enough for the saucer's clinking to correspond with the sight of her lowering it to the table.

"Sometimes I have difficulty sleeping—," he said, yawning and then leaning over to take the cup. "Thank you, Margeaux—though I have more problems battling the administration than I do my insomnia."

The slender feline peered at him with her one luminous and one dark eye. "What kind of problems?" she asked.

"They won't give me the 3deo platform I asked for, and they balked at the mere mention of the overnight."

"An overnight?" Margeaux glanced over her shoulder from where she stood at the sofa, folding the afghan.

"Sure," Kellen said, fingers curling around the handle of the mug. "Intensive history lessons! Ardent discussions! Games! Food! And stars." He grinned. "It makes the text more meaningful when you can see Sol's light, no matter how faint."

"It sounds wonderful," the girl said, thin tail curling around her ankle. She patted the folded afghan, then sat on the floor in front of the center table. The base of

'Mortal Coil' scraped the table-top as the Karaka'An feline turned it. The hairs on the back of Kellen's neck rose.

"Mr. Grove, what did you study when you were in school?"

He rubbed the back of his neck, smoothing the hairs down. "A few things. Recently, history, with a masters in biomedical ethics."

"Biomedical ethics," Margeaux murmured. "That hardly seems connected with history."

"Think about what you've been learning the past few weeks and see if you can repeat that."

Margeaux's ears sagged and she smiled at him with chagrin. "I don't think I could." Her pale brows furrowed. "I just can't imagine spending two years talking about biomedical ethics. Is there really that much to say?"

"Oh, you'd be surprised," Kellen said, chuckling. "You could spend years discussing the ethical implications of the gengineering of the Alliance's races. The catalog of diseases alone was enough to set my head spinning, and we had to memorize them all."

"How many of them are there?" the girl asked, eyes widening.

"Oh, enough. Some one hundred and forty three still prevalent."

"How do you memorize that many diseases?" asked Margeaux, openly staring at him.

Recollections of late nights at coffee houses made Kellen grin. "We had a sort of chant that put them in alphabetical order. Aminerrea, Auregh-Rosen Syndrome, Balanatus, Beritt's Disease, Buliat, Cermoniah. . . ."

"Those all sound so funny," she murmured. "Auregh-

Rosen almost sounds like a person."

Kellen laughed. "It does, doesn't it? It's an interesting one, too. Auregh-Rosen causes people to be born partially or fully deaf, thanks to the haphazard way some of the engineers handled ears for the early versions of their creations. You remember from your text that we weren't created Seersa and Karaka'An?"

Margeaux nodded, her fingers still caressing the sculpture's base. "Racial distinctions came later, when we segregated on board the ships and that segregation enhanced physical characteristics through artificial selection."

"Very good. You've been doing your reading." Kellen leaned forward, sliding his half-emptied mug onto the table. "The first scientists wanted to give us animal ears and the increased directional sensitivity that came with them, but weren't sure, as they weren't about anything at that point, how to slice the human ears out of the equation. They had to find a way for our essentially human brains to accept and process the information supplied by the abnormal ears. As it fell, they couldn't even figure out how to stop the constructs from being born with two sets of ears. In fact, we all have vestigial human ears."

Margeaux touched the base of her pointed, feline ear self-consciously. "We do?"

"Yes! They're called Auregh-Rosen processes." Kellen waved her over, captured one of her hands as she kneeled at his feet. He felt along his jaw until he found the knob and then pressed her slim fingers to it. "There. Feel it?"

Unfocused, bicolored eyes stared past him as she fumbled along the edge of his jaw until her fingers separated the slight bump from the rest of his skin.

"Oh!" she glanced at him, eyes large and mouth loose. "I didn't know!"

"People with Auregh-Rosen Syndrome are throwbacks to those early constructs. The symptoms range from having a larger cartilaginous lump to having nerves unable to process the augmented information from animal ears. You can be partially deaf or have four fully developed ears. It's an interesting syndrome, and a milder one though often associated with more unpleasant complications."

"Do I have one of those knobs?" Margeaux asked, still touching the tiny lump below his temple.

"Most certainly. Ninety percent of all the Karaka'An and Seersa do. Here, come with me." Kellen strode to the mirror, motioning her in front of him. He placed his hands on her cheeks and gently tilted her head forward and to the side, then brushed through her short, soft hair. "Let's see . . . ah, yes. Actually, yours is better defined than mine." He ran his fingertip along the outside edge of the lump, then pulled the wisps of pale honey-brown hair back behind it so she could see.

"Oh!" Margeaux's eyes studied herself in the mirror intently, her hand rising. Kellen steadied her head in his right hand, his left holding back her hair as she caressed the bump. "How . . . how strange!"

Kellen chuckled. "The events have passed, but the evidence remains." He watched her fingertips graze the edge of the process, and with a lingering smile lifted his eyes.

His hands, large and white, one with fingers splayed

to hold up her head, the other cupping a neck almost as slender as his wrist, in a position as intimate as an embrace . . . . her body only inches from his, defining its slopes with the warmth emitted from beneath a thin tunic . . .

Her tail, at its base, pressed against his hips.

Kellen stiffened.

"So does it mean anything that mine is bigger than yours?" Margeaux asked anxiously, twisting to face him.

Grateful that the black skin on the inside of his ears masked the blush, Kellen replied, "The size of the process is basically random." He grinned. "You haven't noticed being deaf, have you? Unless you have, there's nothing to be worried about."

Margeaux giggled, relieved, before returning to her chores.

An hour later, Kellen sat on the couch in his den, one heavy foot propped against the coffee table. Nervous fingers drummed a beat against the butt of the armrest, and his mouth stretched in a tight line across his demi-muzzle. The thumb and forefinger of his free hand slowly sawed against one another where they rested against his thigh.

Behind his black ruffs, the track of her soft fingertips where they'd rubbed across his jaw burned. He could still feel her neck against his bare palm, the artery that had chafed his skin with its regular pulse.

"Hey!" Joet called cheerfully as the door slid open, and just as quickly, "Ho . . . you look disturbed." The foxine tossed his teaching aides on a nearby chair and dropped onto the sofa next to Kellen. "Why the face, there, *arii*?"

"The usual dark thoughts," Kellen said, forcing a grin.

"More specifics, please." Joet poked him in the side. "I'm used to the long faces you wear when you're thinking generally dark thoughts. This one looks different."

Kellen grimaced. "Well, there's this student. . . ."

"Mmm-hmmmm . . ."

"And she . . . well, she's a nice girl, but. . ."

"Ohhhhh, the light dawns," Joet said, grinning. "She's got stars for you."

Kellen grimaced; it wasn't quite the truth, but then . . . he wasn't sure what had happened downstairs, or why it was still affecting him. "So have you had this problem?"

"Who me?" The Tam-illee laughed. "Being so handsome, the girls swoon over me all the time!"

Kellen's glare elicited a chortle from Joet.

"Seriously," said Joet, "Yes, I've had a few. My only advice is to be gentle with them. They usually never see that they're being rejected until they've found some guy their own age to fixate on, and then you can relax."

The black foxine smiled. "Thanks. I'll try it."

Joet chuckled and stood, clapping a hand on Kellen's shoulder. "You do that. Don't lose any sleep over it, hey?"

Kellen frowned, then spoke quickly, interrupting the smooth motion of the Tam-illee turning from him. "Actually, Joet, there's something more important I needed help with. It's about borrowing the amphitheater . . ."

In the utter black of the windowless room, gray eyes opened and Kellen gasped. His chest heaved under the sheets, its rhythm slowing as he focused on the wall. A fleck of pink glinted in the mirror as he licked the salt off his lips before it dripped onto the pillow. He hadn't had the nightmare in two weeks, hadn't dreamed of the obscene ropes, like sickly umbilical cords.

"Margeaux," he muttered. Her fingers, turning the base of the figurine. Her fingers on his jaw. Her neck.

Her vestigial human ears and odd eyes and so-thin tail.

Kellen sat up and drew his legs over the edge of the bed, propping his hands against the mattress. Gingerly he rotated his head until it faced the corner, eyes squeezed shut as the muscles gripped his throat and upper shoulders. Caressing the hollow of his throat against the discomfort, the Seersa levered himself back onto the mattress, staring at the ceiling. His thighs and first calves twitched, too tense to relax. Kellen attempted to compose himself for sleep.

Ten minutes later, he rummaged through his bureau drawers and slipped back onto bed, propping himself up against a mound of pillows. The data tablet in his hand illuminated the contours of his face with a phosphorescent green light that rendered his pupils opaque. The words 'Accessing U-banks' flashed steadily on the upper left hand corner of the screen in response to the swift motions of his fingers, and he waited, ears pressed to the back of his skull. As the search status indicator turned, an awareness of his own body flooded him. Seersa. Primary DNA Source Human, Secondary DNA Source Vulpine, Tertiary DNA Source Feline. Nominal Body Frame A. Digitigrade, Primary Load-bearing Member Muscular.

Four digits, claw bed type 2. Jaw and lower facial structure Demi-Muzzle Stratum 2. Coat Pattern Recessive Feline Bicolor.

So normal on the outside. He met the original specs.

The tiny screen on the data tablet blanked, then filled with images along the left side with text marching down the right. A beautiful Seersa woman, ruddy with black 'socks' and mouth and throat danced in one, cast a startled glance at the viewer in the next, taught a student in a third.

"Valarie," Kellen murmured, his whisper infringing on the silence. The windowless cube of his room suddenly stifled, too insulated.

He could not bring himself to read her current biography. Flicking the data tablet off and dropping it to the floor, Kellen slid deeper into the sheets. He slept poorly.

"This way, don't crowd!" Kellen leaned back against the jamb as the class clotted at the door to the science department's 3Deo amphitheater. His ears twitched, tracking his students' mystified whispers. Margeaux was the last to file through the door into the dark and he entered behind her, peripherally aware of the heat of her body and determined, angrily, to ignore it.

The Seersa said, "Spread out . . . there. All right. I'm sure you're wondering why we're here today instead of in class."

"After half the madcap mischief you've chased us on, Mr. Grove, we wouldn't be surprised if you flew us to the moon," Rachel interjected, only her teeth and the whites of her eyes showing in the dark.

Her comment met with low, good-natured laughter and Kellen grinned; he liked the way his class relaxed instantly in his presence. "Why thank you, *arii*, but I'm afraid we're not due for any such exotica here. As some of you might know, the Tam-illee are celebrating their landing on Tam-ley all this week with festivals. While I can't arrange a field trip, I did manage to get a sop tossed our way . . . so if you'll relax, I'll roll the film."

A few hushed murmurs traveled the room, but Kellen detected no alarm or undue curiosity. They had no idea yet what he'd managed to arrange.

With a grin that showed a little more tooth than usual, Kellen said, "Computer, establish feed." He braced one hand against the wall.

The raucous sounds of thousands of people laughing, talking, singing vaulted from around the room while pipes knit the cacophony together with music spun from breathy stringed instruments. A throng leaped into existence in the chamber, dancing around a squat platform. Wooden poles trailed colorful ribbons braided into stylized helixes as the dancers passed around and through bewildered students whose bodies had suddenly acquired the patina of an alien sun's light.

Above them, in the fullest radiance of that light, a figure on the platform led the merry-makers: a lithe woman splashed in only the softest white light and wearing a silver, footed body-suit. As she pirouetted, the layers of her gauze skirt hugged her ankles as if twirling through water. In one hand, she carried the mask of a true arctic fox, like the one whose blood had endowed her with her beauty despite generations of interbreeding; in the other, the eyeless mask of a human. She danced in a world beyond the music and the noise of the crowd.

Kellen had paid four of his four and a half weeks of salary to buy an hour's live feed from the Touchground Festival on Tam-ley. Watching the complex emotions unraveling on the faces around him, he thought he'd cheated the salesman.

"Was it real?" Margeaux asked later, draped on the sofa and hugging one of the afghans to her chest. Her eyes, rounder than usual, fixed dreamily on the wall as her tail tip drew lazy circles on the cushions.

Kellen chuckled as he checked off notes for the sophomores' upcoming quiz. "If you're talking about the Festival, then yes . . . and if you're talking about the fact that you witnessed a small piece of it, well, yes again. If you're talking about something completely unrelated, I'm afraid you'll have to be a little more specific. Physics . . ."

" 'Isn't your field', I know, I know," the girl said, giggling. "You always say that. Why?"

He shrugged, then grinned at her over his tablet. "It's true." The sudden flop of her tail onto the ground grabbed his attention. "So, are you going to be useful for real work today, or are you going to just lie around?"

Margeaux's pointed ears blushed a delicate coral pink. She buried her nose in the afghan and said, "Mr. Grove, I . . . thank you. I've always wanted to see something like that. I never thought I would."

"You haven't, really. Not yet," said Kellen. "I went to

the Touchground on Tam-ley two years ago. It was overwhelming. You'll have to plan to go one day."

"Maybe," Margeaux said, but her reply lacked conviction.

Kellen started to tease her and lost the words when the door slid open for Headmaster Darteriov.

"Mr. Grove! It has come to my attention that you have made illicit use of the science department's resources."

He put aside the data tablet and rose to his feet. "I would hardly call it illicit, lady. I obtained permission from Joet Starsteps, who, as I understand it, is responsible for scheduling the amphitheater's use."

Darteriov stared at him so intently he almost felt dizzy. The relief when she broke off her stare to transfer it to her data tablet almost tumbled Kellen back to his seat. He felt extreme pity for the tablet.

Staring down her broad demi-muzzle, the cheetaine read aloud, " 'Headmaster. My son has just told me about an excellent experience he had in one of your history classes. I've never heard him so interested in history before. Thank you for taking steps to reform your curriculum.' " She redirected that stare at him and said, "That is the second transmission I've received today. Correct me if I am wrong," her voice still clipped, "But we released the students only half an hour ago."

"That is . . . correct, yes, Headmaster."

Darteriov stared at him for another full minute; then she tucked the tablet beneath her arm and said, "Very well, Mr. Grove. You'll find your future requisitions filled. Within reason, of course. Good evening."

Kellen dropped into the chair the moment the door

shut behind the Harat-Shar, concentrating so hard on regaining his breath that Margeaux almost stopped his heart when she spoke.

"Is she . . . always that intense?"

Kellen slid his hand over the back of his neck, then chuckled. "Yes."

A shiver rippled down the girl's spine. Her odd-colored eyes peeked at him from over the mounded afghan. "Does this mean we get to have the overnight?"

The thought hadn't even occurred to him. A grin spread over Kellen's mouth. "Why, yes. I suppose it does."

"Be careful," he called, one hand grasping the cool rock. "The path crumbles near the top of the fall. Watch your feet!"

A chorus of replies tumbled down to him with the splash of the water. Living in a building insulated from the sound had almost erased the water's music from his memories. Kellen paused, shading his eyes against the setting sun. A bright spark wafted in lazy circles above their destination and he grinned, wishing briefly for wings to match his Phoenix student's.

Tugging the shoulder strap on the sack, the Seersa clambered after his class. The broad wedge of his foot reported the damp give of the autumn soil and the occasional sharp edge of a young pebble. Cool air bit the inside of his nostrils: sharp, clean, and pungent with the scent of moss and earth.

Several minutes later, he arrived at the top of the low, rocky hill. The stream that fed the fall issued from a grass-felted depression, its source lost in the short wall of the mountain. A narrow bridge connected the thin strips of rock that framed the precipice where the foaming waters plunged to the pool beneath Silvergate.

Kellen dropped his sack on a rock near the center of the green bowl. "Remember, if you want to explore, be back in an hour and be careful. The Headmaster won't kill you if someone gets hurt on this trip—she'll kill me."

A few chuckles and the students dispersed; he doubted many of them had been up the short slope. Curious himself, Kellen keyed the shield around the sack to keep inquisitive creatures from their food, then decided on a likely direction.

Half an hour later, he'd decided he'd been missing life in the extreme south of the continent. Kellen crouched on a rock and closed his eyes, steadying himself with large hands as he pulled in a long breath through his nose. He could almost believe he'd preserved the ability to truly smell the way the foxes that comprised some small measure of his genome could. The thin white trees standing beside him curled hooked and spindly fingers into the sky, defining the cool shadows that striped his body. He opened his eyes to add sight to the sensation of the coppery light streaming from the west. A soft smile curved over his mouth, and he hopped off the rock to follow the song of the water.

Several paces down the trail, the stones jutted from the soil in irregular patterns, and several sturdy trees had fallen across the fall. Perched on one of those trees, dangling her feet in the water, was Rachel. He waved to her.

"Are you sure you've got a firm seat?"

"Oh, yeah, Mr. Grove! This is fantastic. Come on out!"

"I'm not sure," he said, eyeing the cold foam, "If I fall in, it'll take me a lot longer to dry off."

She only grinned and waved again, so he shrugged and crawled awkwardly out to join her. The digitigrade jointing of his legs might have served their animals better for such activities, but for someone basically bipedal they were not ideal.

"Oh my," Kellen said when he finally secured his perch. The mountains beyond Silvergate's premises rose through a mysterious brown and forest-green vista, veiled by a fog of water tinted sparkling bronze. "Rachel, this is quite a throne you've found yourself."

"Thanks," she said, grinning. She sat with her back facing his side, straddling the trunk and teasing the crests of the waterfall with her toes. "Say, Mr. Grove . . . there's one thing I can't figure."

"Go ahead," Kellen prompted when she fell silent, her dark eyes studying one of the pools created by a tiny dike of rock.

"See, I really, really believe that what we did was wrong. Really wrong. It's not just that religious thing, you know, playing God. It's . . . well, it's that we were making people, real people with real feelings, without knowing how. And to do that, without being able to give them the same things any normal human is born with . . . it was wrong." Rachel scraped the white bark of the tree with her blunt fingernail. "But, Mr. Grove, I wouldn't want to live in a world where there was no Alliance. No Seersa and Karaka'An and Tam-illee and crazy Harat-Shar and

Naysha, and . . . God, look at what we made! I can't imagine life without the Pelted."

Kellen paused, surprised at the vehemence of her words.

Rachel looked at him, distraught as she rarely showed herself to be in class—but honest, as always. "I can't reconcile it, sir. How can I be happy about something that's wrong?"

"I know how you feel," Kellen said. He propped a foot up on a limb that had lost most of its length in the storm that had also deprived it of roots. "After all, if the humans hadn't meddled, I wouldn't be alive." He flicked an ear. "I'll tell you something, Rachel. I shouldn't, since you're supposed to arrive at your own answers, not accept mine. But still. It's a given that people make mistakes, right?"

She nodded.

"Or that people sometimes intend to do horrible things."

Again, she nodded.

"But good sometimes arise from horrible acts. It doesn't make those acts any less reprehensible, but it might, just might redeem them. Why do you think the humans did what they did?"

Rachel paused, then said, "I think they were lonely. Even the ones who bought those first models for . . . companionship . . . they could have masturbated or something. So . . . yeah. I think . . . we just wanted to be less alone."

Kellen dipped his head. "I think so too. Are they less alone?"

"Yes!"

"And are there billions of people alive today who wouldn't be otherwise?"

"Yeah."

Kellen spread his hands. "That's all I can offer you."

The human returned her gaze to the falling water, wisps of her black curls floating in the cold breeze generated by its motion. "I'm not sure that's very comforting," said she after a few minutes, "Though I guess there's nothing wrong with being lonely. I only wish . . . well, we'd been more careful about it. More . . . humane."

"You can't change the past."

"No," Rachel said, then turned a lopsided grin on him. "I guess we're the dopey romantics of the galaxy. Not wise enough for the brains in our heads."

"If that's so," Kellen said, grinning back, "Then it must be genetic, because you passed it on to the rest of us."

She chuckled and twisted to throw her arms around him. "Thank you, Mr. Grove. I'll do some more thinking."

"Just so long as you don't accompany the thinking with leg-breaking, I'll be happy. You still have twenty minutes or so."

"I'll be there. I wouldn't miss the talk for anything!"

Kellen climbed off the tree, leaving the girl curled on its center. He stretched his toes across the cool soil and smiled. The trees and rocks had seemed merely welcoming before; now they were positively radiant.

Halfway up the trail he paused to rest, one hand splayed across a rock. When he pulled his fingers away, a non-reflective smear drew his eyes. One glance at his thumb revealed a nick in the skin, welling a bead of blood as smooth and round as a ruby cabochon. One of the sun's dying rays pricked a highlight off its surface.

A curse escaped him. He spent several minutes cleaning the rock, another patching the cut with the pocket medisealer that accompanied him everywhere.

The fire cast a ruddy light against the purple twilight. Arranged in an informal circle, Kellen and his students toasted the chunks of meat, vegetables and tangy cheese he'd brought as their light supper. He studied each of them, as accustomed now to their eccentricities as they were to his. It was only natural that Derrick, the Hinichi wolfine, sat so straight his posture seemed affected. Cyclone's metallic feathers reflected both fire and sky where he lounged beside Richard, the human male who rotated his meat with an intent expression. Rachel had returned from her contemplation with a drowsy, thoughtful expression; she rested against a pillow beside Madeira, the reedy Aera girl. Donegan with his good-natured, handsome face reclined beside Julia, the human girl whose interest in biology often pointed classroom discussions in unusual directions. The drowsy Asanii male, Bernard, leaned back on his palms, occasionally poking the Harat-Shar pantherine Una in the side.

Margeaux had claimed the spot nearest him, lying on her stomach on a smooth, long rock, one slim arm folded under her chin, the other stretched to toast her cheese slice.

"I brought games," he began, but Rachel interrupted. "No games. Tell us stories!"

Madeira nodded vigorously. "I want to know about Joy, and Holly."

"We're not supposed to cover the Revolution in this class," Kellen said, stopping when they groaned.

"Tell us the stories," Donegan said, his eyes flat with reflected firelight.

He could no more deny such a request than he could stop breathing. What was history, save stories? True stories, the best kind? As Kellen leaned forward to weave the words, he realized how precious this role had become to him. It had not been so important in the beginning, when he'd chosen it nearly at random, as flight from pain and denial.

As the sky darkened around the stars, Kellen spun the stories of the Origin. Told of Dr. Shandlin and Joy, the first creation ever to live beyond the test tube, the sweet girl more fox than human whose mind had never ripened past the bewildered happiness of a three-year-old child's . . . all the tales he'd heard about the first construct, corroborated from Shandlin's journals when Earth had met at last the fruits of her forgotten work.

There could be no justice done to such a being, save to speak only the truth. By the time Kellen ran out of truths to tell about Joy, no blue remained in the sky and the stars provided the only light.

"Okay," he said, rubbing his throat, "Let's look for distant suns while I give my throat a rest."

They shook themselves reluctantly from their trance, following Kellen as he grabbed a canteen of water and trekked to the waterfall's bridge. Resting against the wooden banister, the Seersa searched the sky, orienting himself, then pointed. "There . . . see the Almost Star?"

The star almost exactly due north was also the brightest. While they located it, Kellen swallowed a quick mouthful of water, parched tongue poking into the dry recesses of his mouth. He should have known better than to let his mouth get that way, when the smallest cut had to be sealed. "Look just to the right of it. There should be a tiny light between the Almost Star and that rather large reddish blob. It's pretty faint, but if you stare long enough you'll see it."

A soft breeze tugged at his black jaw ruffs. Kellen closed his eyes to enjoy the cool wind's fingers.

Rachel's voice: "Is that it?"

Kellen roused himself, taking a deep breath. "That's it. Terra's sun."

Their murmurs brushed his ears so softly he almost lost them to the song of the falling water; their bodies told a more complete tale, the tension in their limbs, the tilted heads. He felt it himself, a tiny dark of yearning and pain pushing at the base of his ribs.

"It's so small," Una's murmur, twisted by wonder.

"But it's not. Is that what you're trying to say?"

At least three pairs of eyes found his, wide and white.

Born too low in his throat for mirth, Kellen's chuckle sounded closer to a growl. He raised his own eyes. "No matter where we're born," he said, some of that ancient hunger opening his throat, "No matter where we go, or how many generations and light-years separate us from that earth, it is our home. More than our birth planets, more than the Alliance core itself. That is where we were made, and we all know it . . . young and old. There's no denying the call."

"But we left," said Margeaux. She turned her eyes from the sight of Sol. "Holly led us away. Earth might be our birthplace, but we've grown up and moved on."

"How can you ever move on from something like that?" Donegan wondered, his voice hushed. "From the knowledge that you were made? That you and everything you know started so small?"

"Tell us about Holly," Margeaux said, her bicolored eyes fixed on his.

"If I told you all the tales of Holly, we wouldn't be here until dawn. We'd be here until the end of the world," Kellen said, smiling. His hands flexed on the wooden banister behind him. There was something too intense about Margeaux's stare.

"Anything. One story."

"One story." His gaze rose to Sol's light as if drawn. "You know that Holly's diaries didn't survive the diaspora."

"I didn't," said Richard. They were all looking at him now.

"Holly purportedly kept a diary about her life, beginning the day she learned to write," Kellen explained. "On the journey out it was accidentally destroyed, yet we have more documentation about the events leading up to and following the revolution and diaspora than we do about any other part of our origin. When we met humanity some three hundred years ago, they only added to that knowledge." He paused for breath, a dark ache in his chest. "That there are so few of Holly's original words remaining is a shame. But we do have a few of her public speeches and one or two private conversations on record. There's even a song that draws on some of those private conversations where she discussed how she felt."

"Can you sing it, Mr. Grove?" Donegan said.

"There are so many songs about her. Not so many about her feelings," Una murmured.

Margeaux only stared at him with her one bright and one dark eye.

Kellen pushed away the ache and sang.

> *There are more stars in the sky at night*
> *than Joy was taught to count.*
> *And I must somehow lead our flight*
> *even though it's tantamount*
> *to suicide, they tell me. Suicide.*
>
> *How can we ride each other's hopes*
> *when so much could go wrong?*
> *When it's on Terra that Wolf lopes,*
> *and Lion sings her eerie song,*
> *to these stars, I've heard her. These stars.*
>
> *But what greater prize than freedom must*
> *we follow to that light?*
> *What greater price than true-home, what*
> *ransom more than Right?*
> *What greater love and hunger drives me on*
> *despite my fears?*
> *When all I know and touch and change may*
> *end with frigid tears . . .*
> *May end with frigid tears.*

I have seen the ships they've built us now
have walked inside their skin.
We'll know them when we fly them, and how
to put to dreams our kin:
Another risk, they tell me. Another risk.

Waking schedules have been fixed and fit
to last the hungry days,
A long and lonely watch to sit
as the months grow long and gray,
and tumble into decades. Into centuries!

But what greater prize than freedom must
*   we follow to that light?*
What greater price than true-home, as we
*   spread our wings for flight?*
What greater love and hunger drives me on
*   despite the pain,*
That drags at me and leeches, leaves me
*   solemn in the rain . . .*
Leaves me crying in the rain.

But I have dreamed the future—who but me
*   can paint those dreams?*
I have dreamed the future, and it's nothing
*   like it seems.*
It's full of toil, of strife and vice,
of love and joy . . . and sacrifice.
Oh! I have dreamed the future, and there's
*   freedom in those dreams.*

There are more stars in the sky at night
than my naked eyes can see.
And I must absolutely lead our flight,
even if destroying me
is the price. Is part of that price.

What greater prize than freedom must we
*   follow to that light?*
What greater price than true-home, in ex-
*   change for truthful sight?*
What desperation drives me on, nightmares
*   tearing me from sleep,*
That claw at me and ride my back and slash
*   me 'til I weep . . .*
And watch me as I sleep.

Kellen faltered, aware again of his surroundings, of ten pairs of eyes fixed on him.

"Those were her words?" Madeira whispered finally.

"Most of them," he said, clearing his throat and rubbing its base with a white thumb. "They were pieced together from separate conversations." He smiled faintly. "I'll go back and brew our hot cocoa. There'll be a pot waiting on the warmer, but feel free to stay here as long as you like. Joet Starsteps lent me his locator . . . ," he dug in his pocket and offered the card to Donegan, "So if you want to know more about the local stars, use it. We're near many of the Core worlds. Their suns should be easy to find."

He left them to star-gaze, rubbing the dark space under his chest. Upon reaching camp, he placed a foot against the flat stone and propped an elbow on a knee, massaging his forehead.

"You wrote it, didn't you," a soft soprano said.

Startled, Kellen glanced into the fire-lit face of Margeaux. "*Arii . . . ?*"

"You did. You said you weren't a musician." She sounded wistful. "But you sing so well. Like a real singer, a trained singer. And you talked about the song as if you'd written it."

His dark ears burned, but the blush was less embarrassment and more shame, anger. Kellen looked away.

"Why aren't you doing that? Being a musician?" Margeaux stepped closer, her footfalls hardly sounding against the damp ground. She captured the hand dangling over his knee, her tiny fingers rubbing along the edges of his larger ones. Goosebumps ran from his neck to the base of his spine. "You'd turn the worlds over."

"It wasn't that good."

"Yes it was! It was beautiful. It was. . . eerie." The slim girl shivered, her fur rippling in the reddish light. "Mr. Grove . . . why? Why didn't you do it?"

"The world needed another history teacher." He tried to ignore the sensation of her soft, furless skin chafing against his palm.

"You could have been both. A history teacher and a musician. Everyone remembers songs. I've never heard that one about Holly. No one has heard anything about Holly except that she was brave and strong and sure and fast, and more heroic than anyone ever."

He looked at her. "The world needs heroes."

"Not if it makes everyone believe they could never be

one," Margeaux said earnestly, staring up into his eyes. He found it hard to concentrate on just one of them, wanting to switch from the lime-colored side to the dark green. "Mr. Grove! At least do it a little on the side!"

"You're walking in dreams, girl, if you think that teaching doesn't take all my living energy."

"But your hands, your voice were made for it," she insisted, both her tiny hands cupping his. "You could play piano, or wachitvi—"

"Enough!" He jerked his hand from between her palms.

Margeaux stepped back once, her balance precarious, her expression stunned, reflecting back on him the violence of his countenance.

Kellen clenched his hands and then forced them to relax at his sides. More quietly, he said, "Enough, Margeaux."

Another backward step, and then she fled to the bridge to join the others. Kellen watched her go, forced himself to relax the rest of his body, muscle by muscle. When he finished, he almost wept. He bent to the fire instead and began to brew the hot cocoa.

The day after the overnight dragged on so long Kellen could hardly believe when it ended. He rested his arms on the top of the sofa-chair and laid his head on them. He hadn't slept the night before; like Holly's, his nightmares had become too vigilant. The data tablet slid from his limp hand to fall with one bounce on the dark green cushion. Just a few more minutes and he'd be up-d.

ove."

k stiffened instantly, and he pushed himself upright. "Margeaux," said he, keeping his voice even, "I think I'm too tired for afterschool tod—"

"I wanted to apologize," she said.

The slim Karaka'an feline with the ivory pelt walked to him as he turned from the chair, and Kellen found her under his nose before he could retreat. Tendrils of soft blonde hair framed her face, lashes the same color fringing her eyes, such strange, intent eyes. Her distress marred their shape, brows thin, furrowed. She smelled like strawberries.

"I pushed too hard. It was wrong. I'm sorry. Will you please forgive me? Please."

When he gave no reply, she pressed on, "I can . . . I can drop out of afterschool if you want. Just say you're not angry with me."

"I . . . Of course not," Kellen said when he found his tongue. Worry he could have understood, but the sag of her shoulders, the dead hang of her slender tail, the smell of the oil-sweat rising above the scent of strawberry evoked a far more profound despair. "You didn't mean any harm, Margeaux. I took no harm." A lie, but she needed it so badly. He bent down to kiss her forehead.

She lifted her face and met his lips with her own instead. Her arms wound around his neck, her small body stretching against his. His shock at her audacity left Kellen completely unprepared for her ardor. He could feel her heart beating through her mouth, and she took advantage of his slack jaw to slip her tongue between his teeth and pull his head down to hers.

It took him several breaths to recall himself and jerk away, already searching for words to diffuse the situation, only to realize that her trembling had become sobs. Feeling whiplashed by the sudden shift in her demeanor, he looped his arms around her back.

"Margeaux?" he asked, ears burning beneath their black skin. He certainly hadn't initiated the kiss—he definitely hadn't initiated the kiss!—but nevertheless he said, "I'm sorry. I've obviously overstepped my boun—"

"Why?" she asked him suddenly, her voice muffled by her tears. "Why? Why did they do it? Why did they make us? How could they be so cruel?"

"Margeaux?" Truly bewildered now, Kellen stroked her back, one hand cupping her skull. It fit neatly into his palm. He stared at the sight, an image thrown out of perspective, wildly skewed, preternaturally significant. "I don't understand."

"The humans!" She raised her eyes to his, wet beads clinging to her lashes, clumping them together. "Why did they do it, Mr. Grove? Why? They should have killed us and been done with it!"

"I . . . Margeaux, how could you say such a thing?" Kellen said, shock pushing the words past his internal censor. He shook her gently. "You're young, you're alive, you're beautiful! You have so much, so much that's precious."

"Do . . . do you really think I'm beautiful?" she asked, sniffling.

He could feel the slightness of her frame, the bones of one hip pressing against his leg, the crush of her

st his, rising and falling unevenly. His hands
a phantom sensation: her neck from the day
nirror. He thought of stars.

"I think you're very beautiful," Kellen said, wishing it
were a little less true.

Margeaux did not reply, quivering against him. Then,
softly, "Thank you." She backed away from him without
meeting his eyes, her arms wrapped around her chest,
and fled the room.

"Ohhh, Iley. If that isn't the look to top all looks."
Joet flopped onto the couch beside the Seersa. "What
happened to you, ah? Did your overnight not go off well?"

"Oh no. The overnight was fine," Kellen said, schooling his nausea. "I don't even know how I got into this
one, Joet."

"Let me fix us some coffee and then you tell me
what's got you up in knots."

Kellen rubbed his brow. "I don't know if I could stomach anything right now."

The scarlet Tam-illee clicked the roof of his mouth
with his tongue. "That bad, huh? Well, trust me. I know
just the thing." He padded into the kitchen.

Kellen closed his eyes and concentrated on relaxing.
The smell of strawberries and oil had long since become
cloying but he couldn't move for fear of losing lunch and
breakfast. His own tunic and trousers stank of stress-
sweat. He couldn't decide which was worse: the vertigo
of closed eyes or the nausea of open ones.

Ginger tea cut a swath through the miasma of odors.

The cushion sank as Joet sat beside him. Kellen opened an eye to see the Tam-illee fold one leg over the other, ankle on knee.

"You look really bad, Kellen," Joet said, his voice stripped of its usual cheer.

"Oh, God, Joet, I kissed a student!"

Silence surged into the space created by his outburst. Even the waterfall's distant hiss forbade to fill it.

"Damn, that's a bad one," said the Tam-illee, the teasing comment somehow more terrible for its lack of gaiety. He scratched behind one soot-colored ear, then handed Kellen the tea. "Drink. You need it, I bet."

Kellen received the saucer, his hands trembling. He managed a sip.

"Tell me it was one of the seniors," Joet said. "Please. At least most of them are legal. That'll make things easier if anyone finds out."

"I . . . she's a senior. But she's one year under age," Kellen said, then began shaking again. "Joet . . . 'anyone finds out'. . . . "

"What, you think I'm going to tell? You're upset about it, Kellen! If you weren't, I'd be worried. Now tell me the rest."

Kellen fortified himself with another sip, then confessed the entirety of the story to the Tam-illee, leaving none of the chance encounters out. "And then her lips were there, where her forehead was supposed to be, and she was pulling me down and . . . She wanted it. I . . . I was so surprised I didn't even resist."

The silence this time was contemplative rather than oppressive.

Joet rubbed the handle on his cup and sighed. "This is a nasty piece of work."

"What am I going to do?" Kellen murmured, his hands trembling again. "I feel so dirty. Kissing children!"

"She's hardly a child," Joet answered, voice low. "And from the sound of it, you weren't kissing her. She was kissing you, and being pretty definite about what she wanted. A few more months and no one would have questioned her right, though many would have questioned her timing."

"I'm seventeen years older than she is!"

"Yeah," Joet said, still toying with the cup's handle. "It sounds pretty bad on the face of it. But there's no use whipping yourself for a mistake."

"A mistake," Kellen repeated.

Joet eyed him and said, "A mistake. Or not. Maybe both of you will look back later and be glad of the experience."

Kellen stared at him.

The Tam-illee shook his head. "Look, you need to relax. Why don't you sit under the shower jets for a while, get clean? That will help you calm down."

"Yes. I'll do that," Kellen murmured in reply. His hand wobbled as he transferred the cup to the coffee table.

In the bathroom, he leaned against the sink and stared into the mirror. He hadn't seen that expression since . . . since Valarie. He touched his lips and tensed as a throb prompted him to pull down his lip. The skin on the inside seeped a tiny spider's thread of blood. Kellen stared at it, his eyes gone wild. He slumped to one knee, shaking violently, and vomited until his spittle ran clear.

He assigned in-class reading for all his students the following day, unable to rise above his panic. His dreams had strangled him while sleeping; his nausea while awake.

The seniors were scheduled for last period, and between bouts of depression Kellen fretted over how he would handle Margeaux. When the final class change rang, the Seersa stood and faced the door. One by one the students trickled in and he shifted impatiently, finding himself both dreading and anticipating the girl's arrival.

Rachel flew through the door almost before it opened for her. He registered her terror one heartbeat before her frantic words. "Mr. Grove! Mr. Grove, Margeaux's collapsed outside!"

He leaped past the others, hardly seeing them, and almost ran Rachel down as the human sprinted to the end of the hall. Other students, worried or curious, were already gathering around the slender shape twitching helplessly on the ground. Kellen dropped to his knees beside her, horrified, thinking for a moment that he had done it—the blood, the kiss, she'd had an open cut—but the signs were all wrong for Kerriwiht's Disease and it was much, much too soon for it to be manifesting anyway. Old training reasserted itself as he tried to pin Margeaux down with Rachel's help. It looked like she was having a stroke, but why would a young girl . . .

Attenuated body frame A. The bicolored eyes. The

overdeveloped Auregh-Rosen processes. Her hysteria in his arms the day before locked it into place, and Kellen's hands seized her, palpitating the flesh beneath her arms, over her neck.

Joet skidded across the hall. "Kellen!"

"Joet! Go upstairs and look in the bottom drawer of my bureau. There's a special medpack. Bring it!"

The Tam-illee hesitated only long enough to glance at Margeaux's mindless flailing, then he sprang for the nearest stairwell.

"Mr. Grove, what's wrong with her?" Rachel asked, hanging onto Margeaux's legs with Richard's help.

"Later," Kellen said, his fingers feeding him the information beneath the fragile skin of the Karaka'An's neck. "Help me lift her head up. Rachel, how does she eat during lunch?"

"Huh? Not much at all. Lots of vitamins, though."

Vitamins? Or pills? The case in his brain strengthened. Rachel, Richard and Donegan helped him manipulate the Karaka'An into a loose seated position, propped against his body. Her convulsions weakened, and he felt her neck. "Hurry, Joet, hurry," he hissed, closing his eyes. He heard Una and Madeira shooing away curious onlookers, but the racing of Margeaux's heart overwhelmed his awareness.

"Kellen!" Joet dropped to one knee beside him, the pack in his hand. "Kellen, what's going on?"

Ignoring him, the Seersa snatched the pack and flicked it open, hunting. He grabbed an AAP syringe and slid a disk of hemoproxen into it. Switching his fingers on Margeaux's neck for the syringe, the Seersa keyed it, listening to the soft hiss, his body wound into a coil as tortured as Jazeen's statue.

After an eternal moment, the Karaka'An slumped in his arms, her limbs lax. Kellen checked her pulse, fumbled for a medsensor and placed it against her chest. Returning to normal.

"She's okay now," he said to his small audience.

"What happened?" a clipped voice asked, and Kellen glanced up to see his students and Joet had been joined by Headmaster Darteriov. A flood of anger rolled through him.

"What kind of school do you run here anyway?" he snarled, shaking. "If I hadn't had my own medpack, this girl would have died!"

"We have standard packs on every floor," Darteriov replied, ears splaying.

"Standard packs are fine if you have standard kids. One a floor is fine if you don't care if you lose a few while scrambling for it. Damn you to that Harat-Shariin Hell, Darteriov, if this is the kind of school you run because it's certainly not the kind of school you said you ran!"

"I didn't know this young girl had special needs," the cheetaine said, shaken. She didn't even remove her data tablet from under her arm. "If I had, I would have made arrangements. . . ."

"Yes, well, not all people with special needs feel the need to discuss it with the world," Kellen said bitterly.

Darteriov's tail flicked. "If you will instruct us on the appropriate criteria, we will purchase extended medpacks for each classroom."

Mollified, Kellen said, "Fine." He returned his attention pointedly to Margeaux. When he looked up again, Darteriov was gone.

Joet shook his head and stood. "Iley! You've got to be the only person crazy enough to talk to the Headmaster that way, Kellen." The other students looked at the Tam-illee as Madeira knelt next to the group on the floor.

"Mr. Grove can do anything," said she.

"Apparently," Joet said, smiling slightly. "If you need anything, *arii* . . ."

Kellen nodded, and the Tam-illee left.

"What—"

"Ssh," Kellen said, hushing Derrick.

Margeaux stirred weakly against his arm. Her nose and lips left damp trails against his tunic, and her tongue flicked out, running over her mouth.

"Don't talk yet," Kellen said softly. "You're fine."

She nodded once and let her eyes close, breathing shakily. Her soprano sounded thin when she spoke. "I . . . what . . . "

"You had a partial blood clot blocking your carotid," Kellen said softly. "Fortunately it was only partial, and the medsensor said we took care of it before it could do any damage. Do you feel strange?"

"Can't . . . feel m'fingers."

"Which side?"

"Left."

Kellen nodded. "It'll pass."

Margeaux's eyes focused only minimally on his. Her pupils responded sluggishly to the light. "Tired."

"Rest. Help is on the way."

She nodded and sleep claimed her moments later.

His little class kneeled in a ragged circle around him, wearing pale cheeks or bloodless ears.

Rachel said, "Mr. Grove . . . what's wrong with her?"

His gaze traced the lines of exhaustion leading from Margeaux's closed eyelids, then said quietly, "Yuvett's Syndome."

"Then . . ."

"Then she's got one of the original diseases," Bernard said.

"Yes," Kellen said softly.

They sat on the floor at the end of the corridor until the medics arrived; Kellen released her into their arms, describing the incident to the lead healer-assist while the others pushed her away on an antigrav gurney. By the time the halls had cleared, the bell for day's end had rung; his students had dispersed, leaving him alone.

His climb to the suite felt interminable, but when the door slid open for him Joet was sitting on the couch with two filled shot glasses.

Wordlessly, the Tam-illee handed one to him. Kellen took it, sat beside him, and put his feet on the coffee table. At first sip the liquid scalded his tongue and bit his throat.

"I was eighteen," Kellen said. He saw Joet's ear swivel toward him out of the corner of his eye, a fuzzy, indistinct shape. "I'd been studying harp under a Seersa, Valarie Carsen."

Joet murmured, "I've heard of her."

Kellen smiled mirthlessly. "I imagine you have." He continued. "I went on my birthing day for the full workup they give you before you head for college. The blood analysis came back a few days later. I don't know how they missed it when I was born." He rubbed his thumbs slowly against the wall of the glass, eyes cast down. "Positive, as a carrier for Kerriwiht's Disease."

The Tam-illee regarded him steadily.

"I didn't know what it meant, but the healer put it all down for me. No children, unless I wanted them to have the disease or be a carrier. No intercourse without specialized surgery or careful protection. My blood could infect others with the non-genetic strain of the disease." His fingers were too cold. "They gave me a medisealer to carry with me in case I cut myself, educated me on the disease in its fully manifested forms, genetic and non-." Kellen closed his eyes. "I was shocked, of course, but . . . a carrier. I could live with it. I *would* live with it. But during practice a few days later, my calluses broke open. I sealed them immediately and made the mistake of explaining why to Valarie. And . . . I never saw her again. She never returned my calls, and when I went to her studio I found it locked.

"It wasn't that I loved her. But I admired her. She was brilliant in her music and her intellect, clean and bright like a star above atmosphere. To have her turn away from me because of the blood in my veins . . ."

"So you gave up music," said Joet.

"Yes. 'An unnecessary risk', I think I said to my parents. It had finally become real to me. I wondered how things like Kerriwiht's came about. I started studying history in college, particularly Origin history. Because I could live with it, but others couldn't. There were stories that had to be told, just as I had thought there were songs that had to be sung."

"You actually studied all those diseases?" the Tam-illee asked, brows lifting.

Kellen leaned forward, the glass cupped between his hands and elbows on his knees. "I became a healer's-assist with a specialty in Origin diseases."

"Iley!" Joet exclaimed, eyes widening. "You're practically a doctor. Why didn't you go all the way?"

"I thought about it, but the stories are still there. The music is gone, but the stories remain."

"So you knew how to fix the girl. She's got one of them, does she?"

"Yuvett's."

Joet stared at him. "That one usually kills them before her age, doesn't it?"

"Usually," Kellen agreed. He watched the patterns left on the walls of the shot glass as the alcohol slid down them.

Joet did not reply, and Kellen felt no need to break the silence. A dim, sad satisfaction tugged at him; even after learning about his condition, Joet had not moved away from the couch.

"I'm glad you kissed her."

"What?" Kellen asked, disoriented. The events of the day before hardly registered through the fog of today. "Oh, God, Joet."

"No, I mean it." A limp smile crossed the Tam-illee's mouth. "That poor girl . . . who's going to kiss her, or make love to her, or take her to wife? She's probably going to die before most people are even seriously considering those things. At least this way she got a taste of it

... and you, too."

"What does this have to do with me?" Kellen asked.

Joet clapped his shoulder with his free hand, but it was a gentler gesture than the first time he'd done it. His fingers squeezed the Seersa's shoulder. "Yeah. Who's going to settle down with a carrier, or kiss someone who could kill her with a drop of blood? At least you know you can't hurt Margeaux any more than she's already hurting."

Kellen stared after Joet as the Tam-illee stood, glass in his hand, and wandered into his room.

"She's going to be okay, isn't she, Mr. Grove?" Rachel asked, hugging a pillow to her middle.

The 'Ethical Perspectives on History' class radiated depression. They clumped together on the sofas or on the floor, leaning on one another, wrapped up in afghans, even holding hands. Not an ear stood upright on the heads of the Pelted, nor did any humans' eyes sparkle.

"I think so," Kellen answered. He wished he could join them, glanced at his fingers as he rubbed them together, so smooth, no calluses to give resistance.

"It's all different now," Derrick muttered, his wolfine tail sagging behind him. "I mean, not to make your teaching sound bad, Mr. Grove, but it seemed so faraway. Now . . ."

"Now it's real," Madeira finished.

Kellen sighed. He sat on his sofa-chair, pulling an afghan around his body and propping one foot up on the edge of the table. "I know it's hard right now, *arii'sen*. But don't let what you've just witnessed skew the balance. Yes, there are still people who suffer today. But there are billions of people alive today who would not have been. Humanity has its companion and its ally in space, a friend of a type uniquely predisposed toward understanding its parent race. As I told you on the first day of class, there are no easy answers."

"Because, even if it did good, it was a mistake," Rachel said.

Kellen nodded.

"Do you know whether or not she's going to come back?" Una asked in a small voice. "Are seizures normal with Yuvett's?"

He rubbed the edge of the sofa-chair's arm. So tempting to lie . . . but he hadn't become a teacher to shy from speaking the truths his students needed to hear. "Most children born with Yuvett's die before they reach four years of age. Seizures are typical in advanced stages of the disease, but can also occur during earlier periods." Kellen glanced up and, seeing Una's dismay, added, "I'll call her parents tonight and ask after her."

"Maybe we should give her something. Like a get-well gift," Donegan said.

The others nodded, then turned their gazes to him hopefully.

Kellen smiled. "I'll make some kerinne while the rest of you get started."

He watched as they put aside their anxiety and began to talk about cards and presents. Data tablets appeared out of tunic pockets and sashes, and the students bent close together to scan the u-banks for something they could afford with their pooled resources. He managed a wan smile at the ring of subdued concentration, but it faded as he noticed 'Mortal Coil' in the center of their circle, unmoving, standing in for a slim girl who wasn't there.

That evening, Kellen walked down the hall of the Bellwater Hospital, holding a box in his hands. He hadn't changed clothes, determined not to waste any time. The muted sounds of the healers and their assists as they paced the corridors, the chirps and sighs of their machinery, the cold, clean scent of the tile and the fixtures only strengthened his resolve. His call to the Davis household had won him the invitation to the hospital; unlike Margeaux's teary, fearful mother, he had no illusions about the doctor's reported prognosis.

He paused outside the closed door to Room 205 and glanced at the name glowing on the placard. Inhaling slowly, he stepped inside.

"Hello?" a weak soprano asked in the semi-darkness of the room. He spied movement on the bed, an arm sliding across a blanketed midriff.

Kellen walked to her side and said softly, "I hope I'm not disturbing you."

"Mr. Grove!"

The breathy weakness of her voice sent a ripple of alarm through him. He pulled a nearby stool to the bed and sat. "The same," he said, smiling despite the sight his adjusting eyes brought him. "The class sent you a little something. They miss you."

Margeaux's head drooped, fine hair falling around it.
"I miss them, too." She lifted her chin. "They're sending
me away. There's a specialist on Tam-ley who can help
me."

"Dr. Cloudtouch," Kellen said, nodding. "I've heard
good things about her."

"She'll make me better." Margeaux rolled her bottom
lip between her teeth. "She has to. I don't want to miss
school. . . ."

"Maybe we can arrange a live 3deo feed to you, if Dr.
Cloudtouch thinks it won't interfere with her regimen."

The gratitude in the Karaka'An's eyes sickened Kellen.
Reaching onto the bed, he found her hand and squeezed
it. He did not look away as she searched his gaze.

In the quiet of the dark hospital room, Margeaux
whispered, "Mr. Grove, I'm going to die."

A dozen glib replies rose to the seat of his mouth.
Kellen could speak none of them.

Margeaux's fingers clutched his weakly. "I keep thinking about Joy. She only lived five or six years. She could
barely hear or see, or even understand her world. I'm so
much luckier than she was. I keep telling myself that. But
I must be a little deaf after all, sir, because I can't hear it."
She looked down. "I worry about my parents. I hope they
won't feel the same kind of pain Dr. Shandlin did. I don't
want to hurt them. But . . ." Her chest lifted violently and
her voice trembled, tiny in the dark, "But I haven't done
anything yet. The festivals, the worlds, Earth, so many
things I haven't seen . . . and I haven't even had a chance
to decide what I would have done. When I leave, it'll be
almost like I was never here at all."

"Margeaux," Kellen said, forcing the words past a closed throat. He tightened his grip on her hand, touched her face with the other. His fingers came away wet. "Margeaux, Dr. Cloudtouch will do everything she can for you. She's had some spectacular successes. There is a chance, no matter how small, but you won't win unless you fight for it."

"I know," she said, her cheek leaning into the curve of his palm. "But I'm so tired of fighting. Of trying to be normal, when I'm just not. I never will be."

"I understand," Kellen whispered.

She released a long, nearly silent breath. Kellen didn't move, his hand around hers, his fingers cradling her head.

When he realized she'd fallen asleep, the Seersa glanced at the chronolog on the wall. Ten minutes in this silence. Gently, he slid his hands from hers. Leaving the gift on her nightstand, he took himself from the hospital, heading back to the rail that had carried him from Silvergate's depot.

The lights bled past him in a teary stream as he leaned, impassive, against the pole in the center of the empty cab. It was a clear night with only a sliver of a moon to accompany the stars. As he studied them, unmoving above the fluid mobility of the city, a sense of disconnection settled deep into his bones. He flexed his fingers against the pole, pressing smooth fingertips against the cold metal. His vision skewed, then steadied one degree off-axis. When the rail stopped at the downtown exit, he disembarked, drawn by a need he no longer could justify denying.

Hours later, Kellen sat in the empty darkness of his living room. The water outside the window ran black, reflecting only the brightest of the stars. He'd arrived long past midnight to the quiet of his shared apartment, exhausted but emotionally grounded in a way he hadn't been for years. A mug of kerinne steamed on the table. His expanded data tablet, long neglected, patiently blinked on standby. Beside it, the discarded tuning fork lay with the medisealer and a wad of cotton balls.

Kellen closed his eyes, seeking a place that had been abandoned when the nightmares had come. His palms, his fingertips throbbed, sensitized by the memory of her skin, her pelt, the condensation of her breath on the back of his hand. He steadied the new harp propped between his legs, reached for the strings, and embarked on the arduous task of toughening his fingertips. The calluses were long gone, but the music remained.

ROSETTES AND RIBBONS

"**A**ND HERE IS YOUR new room!"

Peli glanced around, brows rising. "Dr. Edisse, do all Aeran edifices look like huts or tents?"

The older Asanii chuckled. "Most of them, yes. A by-product of their culture."

"Nomads, right?" she said, putting down her bag.

"You've been doing your homework."

"Oh, professor, you know I always do my homework!"

Dr. Edisse laughed again and leaned forward to put an affectionate hand on her head. "Yes . . . you were always my star pupil. But you're not a student anymore. Forget that at your own peril! This is the real thing we're working with now, not case studies."

Peli's gaze swept her new lodgings again, the bright fabric walls billowing lightly over the scraggly grass and rising to a rudimentary ceiling; behind her, another wall of cloth served as the separation between her mentor's room and her own. "I don't think it's possible to forget that this is the real thing," she answered, eyes round, "we never had rooms this . . . err . . . transient at the university."

"No, that we did not," the Asanii replied, handing her a data-tablet; Peli tried to figure out which was more out of place, the long tall figure of the ruddy professor, or the slim, asthetic and technological shape of the tablet. "Dr. La'aina is supervising the nearby archeological dig; they think they've discovered some material on some previously unknown myths concerning their religious pantheon. They've brought in her mate, Du'er to investigate. He's a sculptor and a well-known figure in Aeran pre-historical art. They'll be working with you; your assignment is to translate some of the writings they've unearthed. I hope you've brushed up on your Aeran."

Peli felt her back straighten in mock indignation, "Dr. Edisse! There wasn't a Seersa born. . . ."

"That didn't have twenty tongues," he finished, amused, "I know the proverb. I was just making sure you were awake."

She smiled, now in earnest, "I'll give you reason to be proud of me, sir."

The elder felid leaned over and tousled her head-hair. "I know you will, girl . . . so settle in. And remember, the local scientists are throwing us a little formal welcoming-party in a few days."

"The dinner and dance thing, right?"

"Right. Get to it, Miss Argentson."

Peli smiled again as her mentor stepped through the divider to his half of the rectangular tent, then she turned to her bag to unpack. First, the sleeping pad, which she had not thought would be necessary; she was glad she'd brought it anyway, since no furniture had been provided. Did the Aera expect visitors to bring their own furniture? Or did they sleep on the ground?

Peli shook her head, unable to fathom such a thing. She tossed a few pillows on the ground to serve as seats in case someone came to call on her. A low fold-out table, just large enough for her to lean her elbows on and lay her data tablets she set up beside the bed, and then the projecting mirror, a gift from her mother. That she placed beside the table and activated with her toe, watching the slight shimmer that preceded an image of the opposite wall of the tent. Experimentally she flicked her tail in front of it and was gratified to see a white and mottled reflection; the mirror hadn't been damaged on the trip. She set up a light on the edge of the table and the pad for showering across from the mirror.

Some clothes, a few pieces of jewelry she hung on one of the cross-beams holding up the low ceiling, and her brushes and combs she tossed onto the table. Edisse had recommended she bring light clothing, and she was grateful now for his foresight; Selnor had been approaching winter out of its wet and cold autumn, but this on part of Aren summer was at full. Her coat remained in winter-length. She thought about shearing it, but they were only staying two weeks before returning to Selnor, where she'd be glad for the long fur.

Peli kicked up the short head-board on the bed-roll and dropped onto it, propping herself up with her pillows. Unlacing the first few stays of her tunic against the heat, the Seersa foxine nabbed her tablet to check her mail, finding nothing unusual. A note from her parents, wondering how she was enjoying her internship . . . a formal notice from the alumni society of the Xenoanthropological University at Selnor, asking for contributions . . . some junk mail asking her to purchase this or that . . . the latest issue of Comparative Cultures, her professor's (and her own) favorite journal . . . and a short letter from Manager Tasey at the Ani branch of TKI&I, where she'd worked in her off-hours to help pay for her schooling, congratulating her on her recent graduation and thanking her for her service. Her parents first, then Tasey, then she could sit down and enjoy CC, which noted in the byline that this issue included an article by Dr. Edisse about the pottery of the Ciracaana's Mother Cult.

Peli had just finished sending off a reply to her parents when the jingle of the hand-bells outside her tent-flap indicated a visitor. Surprised, she put aside her data tablet and stood, hastily pulling herself into the mind-frame that the tongue of the Aera required.

"While the sands are still, come in," she said, and it was perfectly couched, her mouth negotiating the odd double vowels the Aera favored without difficulty.

Two Aera stepped in, a female and a male with a bundle. Both were near or exceeded six feet tall if she was any judge, which made her feel self-conscious about her own short stature; the female Aera was colored a glorious bright orange and streaked across the muzzle with brown, her mouth and throat a shocking white. Her long ears sported tufts that hung almost to the back of her head and large, golden hoop earrings with thick red stones. The female had arresting blue eyes, the same color as the wrap around her hips that served as her only clothing, wearing her white chest hair in the heavy shag that most Aera favored. The tiny wings at her ankles were white, tipped with brown.

Beside her, the male neared the black of space, completely lacking ventral coloration; he had a furtive air, arms easily folded against his fluffy chest-ruff, green eyes half-lidded and tiny wings folded against his legs. His maroon wrap was shorter, more perfunctory, just as his earrings were thinner.

They were a female-dominated society, Peli remembered. She stood straighter for the female's scrutiny that she would not be dismissed.

"You don't need to speak our tongue," the female said in a surprisingly husky voice, "We speak Universal at the digs, for the most part. I'm Dr. La'aina, Clan Sereon, and this is my mate Du'er."

Peli shifted out of the Aeran frame of mind and switched to Universal. "My given and family-names are Pelipenele Argentson. I am Dr. Edisse's assistant." To her surprise, they didn't ask if she had any other names; but it was easy to forget that hers was the special pleasure and duty of learning other cultures, not the other way around. "I am told I will be working with you. Is that correct?"

"Mostly with Du'er, yes; he will be correlating your translations with any works he will find. Would you announce me to Dr. Edisse?"

"Certainly," Peli answered, determined not to be intimidated by the female. Dr. La'aina infused her slender with so much energy and aggression that she seemed far larger than she was. "If you'll excuse me?"

"Of course."

Peli poked her nose through the separation and found her teacher sitting on his own bed-roll, reading his data tablet. "Dr. La'aina to see you, sir."

"Send her in."

Peli held the tent-flap back for the female Aera, letting out a breath of relief when La'aina swept through, leaving her alone.

"Pelipenele . . . that's quite a mouthful."

The Seersa foxine almost leapt out of her coat. She had forgotten Du'er. "I have an abridged-name, of course," she said, once she regained her composure.

"An 'abridged-name', is it?" he smiled at her, eyes a-sparkle, "You Seersa are so precious, with your quaint little language customs. Will you tell me your abridged-name? We'll be working together a great deal, and I don't fancy having to spit out five syllables whenever I want your attention. I might take to calling you 'vixy' just for relief."

The outrageous behavior and flighty tendencies of the Aera were notorious, and usually explained away by the effects of a nomadic culture. The Seersa supposed it was difficult to grow past the limitations of your own society, if limitations they were; nevertheless she wasn't sure if she liked his mannerisms or not. "You should call me Peli," she said sternly, choosing her words as all her kind did with relentless accuracy.

"Peli it is, then," Du'er said, handing her his bundle, "here are the stone strips we found in the digs."

Peli unfolded one of the skins to peek at the thin, brittle slivers of stone with their scribbled markings; satisfied that they were in mostly good condition and that her assignment would be less trouble than she'd expected, she tied the bundle again and placed it gingerly on the floor beneath her work-table. "Thank you."

"My pleasure. Particularly since it brought me to see you."

Peli glanced at the lazy figure of the Aera male, puzzled. "Pardon?"

"You're a jewel! I've never seen someone so striking. I don't suppose you'd pose for me?"

The Seersa thinned her eyes in complete bafflement. "Pose . . . for you?"

"I don't suppose your Dr. Edisse told you I'm a sculptor? You have a figure that begs for stone. Some of that nice, white stone near the sea-cliffs the Flait hate so, the powder-stone with the sensual crystals would be just perfect."

She was speechless, for once in her life . . . and it wasn't just any life, but the life of a Seersa, the race that provided every premier linguist of the Alliance almost without exception, the Seersa who learned languages with all the facile ease of breathing, the Seersa who took it as a duty to have each of their number add at least five words to their native tongue in their lifetimes and encouraged citizens to add more, if they could. And Peli could find no words.

"It would have to be in the nude, of course . . . such a figure! And the coloration! One would think you one of those barbarian Harat-Shar, except for that face. You have such a delicate nose, beautiful Peli, beautiful Seersa."

Peli almost frothed in her desperate desire to force something out through her throat. What was this maniac *talking* about? Delicate nose? Beautiful figure? Her coloration? Surely he wasn't thinking that she could possibly be the subject for a work of art . . . the very idea was preposterous! She was Pelipenele . . . just Peli . . . not the next Maserinatericktal Kajentarel or Terran Venus de Milo!

The sudden cessation of the low murmur beyond the partition saved her from replying. Dr. La'aina stepped through, followed by the familiar and comforting figure of Edisse.

"You've dropped off the strips?" La'aina demanded of Du'er.

"Of course," he answered smoothly, a smile still quirking at his mouth. His green eyes rested on Peli, who looked away.

"Send someone to the dig when you've discovered something," La'aina said, turning to Edisse.

"I will."

La'aina exited, drawing Du'er in her wake like a magnet. Peli deflated in sheer relief to see them go.

"You look . . . battered," Edisse said, smiling at her gently.

"I feel battered," Peli admitted, dropping onto her bed-roll. "Are all Aera that . . .," she stopped herself from saying 'insane', "that . . . intense?"

"Most of the ones I've met have been, or worse, even."

"Speaker save me!" Peli exclaimed, and Edisse laughed.

"Don't let them get you down in the ears, my girl."

"Of course not, sir."

"Better. I'll be next door if you need me. Next door . . . Next flap?" The elder Asanii shook his head, tail curling in amusement. "No matter. Relax a little and get some rest."

Peli nodded, watching as her mentor stepped back to his side of the tent. She picked up her data tablet to resume her letter-writing and found she could not concentrate. Hesitantly, as if she feared that her reflection had mystically altered in the past twenty minutes, the Seersa placed herself in front of the mirror.

Black eyes gazed back solemnly at her, set in the same lightly furred face she was accustomed to seeing every day while grooming; nothing had changed. Peli studied herself anew, bewildered, trying to see herself with the eyes of the Aera male, but she saw nothing special. Just the same Seersa female, the same four-foot-four, digitigrade Seersa with the long coat, the shoulder-length hair, the long cheek-ruffs . . . the same white body occasionally darkening to a frosty gray where ragged rosettes sprinkled themselves at random, leaving the white untouched save the one perfect black rosette that Du'er could not have seen, hidden under her tunic just beneath her left collar-bone, imprinted there like a permanent decorative pin. No, she was no different . . . so what in the name of the Speaker-Singer had Du'er seen that she did not?

Shaking her head, Peli returned to her bed-roll and took up her tablet — time enough to discover that, once she finished with the day's mail. Then it was to work on those stone strips, a welcome promise of a mystery to be unravelled by her fingers and mind. After that . . . well, she might give a slice of time to the enigmatic Aera.

"Are you going to eat any breakfast at all, girl?"

"Later sir. This is a crucial piece of the text. . . ."

Edisse's voice was bemused. "Would you mind translating, Miss Argentson?"

"Pardon? Oh!" Peli shook herself; so engrossed had she been in the myth that she had spoken in Aeran, not in Universal. "I'm sorry, sir. It's just that I didn't want to break my stride. . . ."

"Which I succeeded in doing, ah? All for the better. You need sustenance! Come here and eat, and if it makes you feel better, give me a report on your progress so far."

Only then did Peli notice the enticing aroma of nut-and-carelberry pastries and warm mocha coffee and milk. She'd been up at dawn, brought from her bed by her own curiosity, a surer alarm than any she'd ever used. That must have been three hours ago, if the quality of the sunlight was any indicator. Peli scrambled through the partition to the mat Edisse had spread on the floor of his room and sat down to breakfast.

"Oh, sir! It's so exciting!"

"Tell me about it, then. Milk in your coffee?"

"Yes please . . . that's enough." Peli leaned forward, cradling her cup in one four-fingered hand. "I spent all of last night putting the stone strips in order. They seem to be numbered in chapters, or volumes. There's only one missing, and a few that are cracked, but most of those are cleanly broken. A little glue will fix them. There's very little lingual shift; according to the Language Archive on Seersana, it's about three hundred years old."

"Not bad, then," Edisse said, popping one of the pastries in his mouth and chewing it deliberately.

"No . . . not at all. It's almost exactly like Modern Aeran, actually. Anyway, I started reading the first strips last night. The first myth concerns three members of their pantheon. Two of them are listed as still known, the females, Taleyira and Seyela."

"The Warrior-Wife and the Warrior-Maiden," Edisse said.

"Yes. But the male . . . well, I can't find any references to him at all. His name is Edera'yn. The story so far is about Edera'yn wooing Seyela, the Maiden. I haven't figured out Taleyira's relationship to Edera'yn yet. This version of the Aeran language assigns the same word to 'enemy' and 'mate', with only a slight inflection to differ it from 'friend' . . . which of course, isn't conveyed in the older Aeran method of writing. They could be any of the three to one another."

Edisse chuckled. "So like the Aera . . . at least nowadays, from what I've read, they differ all three by inflection, instead of just 'friend'."

Peli shook her head. "I don't understand it, sir. How can a culture have the same word for such disparate concepts? You'd think there would be an obvious difference between a mate and an enemy." She finished her first cup and poured herself a new one from the nearby pitcher, then moved on to the pastries, which steamed against her tongue.

"The Aera aren't even the strangest of our comrades

in the Alliance, Peli-pupil." That was a pet name from years ago. "Look at the Naysha, for instance, or the Sire-landers. Even the Harat-Shar and the Hinichi have their oddities."

"I know," Peli replied, "But the Aera . . . they strike me as being especially . . . especially different."

"They're a little harder to deal with, which I think is what you meant to say."

"Well . . . yes, that too."

"It's because they choose to profess that there is nothing important to them." Edisse took one of the after-breakfast mints, leaning back from the mat.

Peli couldn't conceive of such a thing; she was both dismayed by the idea and delighted by it. It was her enjoyment at being surprised and having her mind stretched that had led her to her current profession. "How, how. . . ."

"Self-deluding, we would say," Edisse finished. "When you choose to say that nothing is important to you, more often then not you become unable to choose your priorities, and then everything becomes important instead, blown out of proportion and perspective."

Peli shifted slightly, uncomfortable. "It sounds like a world-view that would create a race of mal-adjusted people."

"You'll have to judge for yourself, my girl. I don't need to remind you to remember exactly what mal-adjusted means."

"No: badly suited for their environment, for their life."

" 'Their' life. Remember that — not for our kind of

living, our kind of cities, our kind of government and society, but for theirs. They might be mal-adjusted to live
as Seersa, or as Asanii . . . but they're not Seersa or Asanii. They're Aera."

Peli nodded, thoughtful.

"Now, if you're done with breakfast, would you like
to walk to the dig with me? I need to discuss a few mat-
ters with Dr. La'aina."

To walk in the sun? See the countryside? Meet the
archaeologists? "Oh, would I, sir! Please, lead the way!"

Edisse chuckled. "Go put something lighter on; you'll
burn up under that tunic. If we were staying longer, I'd
suggest that we both grew chest-ruffs and went around
in native dress, but two weeks isn't long enough for that."

Peli's ears splayed. "I'm not sure I'd be comfortable
walking around half-naked, sir."

"No, you wouldn't, would you?" he laughed, "You
should take some advice from the humans. They said,
'When in Rome, do as Romans do.' "

"I'm not human, sir, and we're not in Rome," Peli replied, knowing that her literal mindedness would evoke a
laugh from her professor, and she was not disappointed.

"Go, girl! We're leaving in five minutes!"

Not long after, Peli was trotting along behind Dr. Edisse, clad in a tunic of blessedly light fabric, raspberry-
colored and cinched at her waist with a silver sash. Her
data tablet rode in a pocket, bouncing against her thigh,
already set to record the results of its passive scanning.
The countryside on this part of Aren was supposedly a
lot like the rest of the continent: arid plains with sparse
dottings of shrubs, rolling in yellow-green to the horizon

where a few orange plateaus splashed with lilac shadows cropped up here and there. The sky was a ruthless blue, shimmering with the heat of the fierce sun. Peli wondered why the Aera bothered to pick up and move their steads at all. There was no escaping the burning regard of that yellow eye, so why expend the energy trying?

The archeological settlement sprang up before them in a series of multi-colored tents in vibrant colors, flaming oranges and stark crimsons, throbbing greens and yellows and purples. Peli grew momentarily dizzy; everything on Aren seemed preternaturally bright, tempting her eyes to water. Beside the tents the excavation was cordoned off with fluttering white sashes. Already people could be seen moving around the site, preparing for the day's labor. Peli counted twelve tents, and four people mobile; she decided while Edisse chatted with Dr. La'aina she would interview some of them, perhaps convince one of them to let her down into the dig.

"I'll find you when I'm ready to leave," Edisse said, interrupting her thoughts, "Meanwhile, enjoy yourself."

"Okay, sir," she replied, and they split off at the edge of the settlement. Peli slowed to study the tents in more detail, pulling her tablet out of her pocket to record the visual aspects. Most of them were pyramidal in shape, with one or two rectangular like the one she shared with Dr. Edisse. The off-world scientists' village where she and the Asanii had been lodged was larger, perhaps twenty-six tents, but they were farther apart. Peli examined the bracing elements of the tents in curiosity. With such a scarcity of wood, she wondered what they used and gasped in interest at the answer. Stone! The Seersa glanced toward the distant cliffs. Perhaps it differed regionally; she wondered if she could send a message on one of the anthropological groups asking if anyone had gathered any data concerning wood-substitutes on Aren.

The female continued strolling along the edges of the settlement, making an arc around the tents that would bring her to the dig. While the study of things past did not interest her half as much as the study of things currently existent, she did recognize that in many ways it was impossible to separate them. Peli drew near the mound of overturned soil beside the growing hole in the earth, skirting it until she came to the white sashes. She peered down into it; no one was working yet.

Disappointed, Peli began to turn.

"So, pretty vixy, when did you say you were bringing your rosettes into my studio?"

Peli reflected that so far, most of her dialogues on Aren had seemed like incidents more properly relegated to dreams: nonsensical non-sequiturs uttered by people completely impervious to reason. "Pardon?"

Du'er was leaning against the mound, body slack with a roguish languor, the tiny wings at his feet moving idly as if to send breezes over his arches and around his ankles. "To be my model. Didn't you say you'd bring your rosettes for me to turn into a work of art?"

The perversion of language never failed to infuriate Peli. Lies, untruths, those things defiled the purpose of the spoken and written word: clear communication. "I never promised you my 'rosettes', nor that I would model for you," she said, carefully enunciating each syllable as if doing so would somehow make more of an impression on Du'er's unmalleable brain.

It was fodder for shock that Du'er actually stood up in surprise, pressing a hand to his chest. "I've offended you with my careless banter!"

"Yes, you have," Peli replied, folding her arms, wondering if he was sincere.

Du'er leaned forward. "Forgive me, beauty . . . but this is a cold and heartless world, with no care for a romantic soul." He leaned back against the mound with an expression of such suffering that Peli was moved despite her nagging suspicion that he was still acting. "Not even my mate understands what touches me. But in you! In you, I thought I saw a kindred soul. I see one still, I think. You must dismiss my way of speaking. It's a defense against most people's callousness."

Peli sighed. He seemed honest, and certainly these didn't sound like the kind of admissions one would lie about. Perhaps he did just want to be friends with her. "Du'er-*alet*," she said, using the more formal word for 'friend' lest she give him ideas, "let us make a deal. I won't tread on your customs if you won't tread on mine."

"But I don't know all your customs!" Du'er protested, dismayed.

"Well, I don't know all yours, either. But I'll tell you one of mine now — don't lie. That's the most important to me. Now, you tell me one of yours."

Du'er paused to think, then said, "Don't reject any of my gifts." He must have noticed her eyes widening, because he held out one hand, "No, I won't give you anything ridiculous, but it is a custom among us to exchange small gifts, once and a while, as tokens of appreciation or gratitude."

Reluctantly, Peli nodded. "Very well."

"Now . . . since you're here, would you like to see one of the statues we unearthed yesterday afternoon? It's quite stunning! Maybe it has something to do with the strips."

Peli's ears swiveled forward in interest. "I'd love to!" She fell into step beside the lanky male, and continued, "Tell me something, Du'er? Why am I translating your stone strips? Don't you have a specialist on the Old Style glyphs?"

"Not one that came as cheaply as you did, beauty."

Peli pursed her lips and didn't reply to that. It was the truth; as an intern, it had cost Aren less to employ her, but it seemed crude to mention it. Then again, she had asked . . .

Du'er lead her into one of the rectangular tents, a dark, eye-mazing azure in color. Pillows with blue and gold stripes were strewn on the floor, plushy and large enough to serve as comfortable chairs, and in some cases, large enough to be comfortable beds. He walked to a table and plucked an object from it, handing it to her.

"Oh," Peli said softly, "It's beautiful!" She turned the figurine over in her hands. It was perhaps a foot tall, slender, made of dark green stone with striations of blue and blued silver punctuated with gemstones. Centuries in the sandy soil of Aren had not substantially marred its surface, or its graceful lines: a stylized Aera female, chin lifted and ears flatly parallel to her neck lifted one hand to the sky and held the other at the height of her shoulders, as if dancing. She wore no clothing, one leg slightly bent as if she had been caught putting weight on her foot. Something in the Aera's lifted hand swirled down, wrapping around her arm, a thin, raised strip decorated with tiny cabochon gems of flitirel and rulent. "What do you suppose that is?" she asked, running a finger over the orange and turquoise gemstones.

"I'm not sure. I was hoping you could tell me about it," Du'er replied, "Perhaps something you've read . . . ?"

Peli shook her head. "Not yet . . . maybe when I get back today, I'll find some clue. Or it might not even refer to the myths at all."

Du'er chuckled, "Don't say such things, beauty! Why don't you take that with you. . . ."

Peli lifted her head to protest, but the male put a finger to his muzzle, eyes sparkling. "Let me finish. Take it with you so that you can see if it pertains to anything you're reading. We've other pieces, but far larger than that one. That's the only one you could carry. It would save you a trip, running to and fro, if you had it with you."

"Are you certain?" Peli asked, ears splaying.

"Didn't you promise not to reject any of my gifts? Well here is one: the gift of borrowed time with this antique. Hold your end of the bargain, dear beauty."

Peli had to laugh. "Okay."

"Peli? Peli? Oh, there you are. I'm ready to go. Good morning, Du'er."

"Good morning, Dr. Edisse," the male replied as the Asanii leaned through the open flap of the tent.

"I'm ready, sir," Peli said, then added to Du'er, "If I find anything I think relates to this statue in the manuscripts, you'll be one of the first to know."

"Not the first?" Du'er asked, mouth quirking.

"That would be a lie," Peli replied good-naturedly, "Since I'd probably have to tell Dr. Edisse about it or burst. He's closer to me, after all."

Du'er laughed, "We should change that, no? Well, have a good morning, beauty."

"You too, Du'er."

"You seem to be getting on well with him," Edisse commented once they left the tent and began the walk back to their settlement.

"We've come to an agreement that allows us to work amicably," Peli answered, handing Edisse the figurine, "I've been charged to hold on to this for a while, to see if anything in the stone strips concerns it."

Edisse studied the statue with professional admiration.

"It must be a very hard stone," Peli added, watching the Asanii's face as they walked amid the scrub-brush, "Otherwise the abnormally high sand content would have had more of an effect on it, I think."

"If this dates to the same time as the writings, it might not be so surprising that it's well-preserved. It's made out of jaen. I haven't seen something made out of jaen since the last time I was in a museum with Aeran artifacts. This is worth a small fortune. Do you think it relates to your myths?"

Peli shook her head. "I'll have to read more. Which I will, after I drink something. I feel parched!"

Edisse handed the figurine back to her with a dry chuckle. "I'm surprised you're not panting . . . I'm sweating up a storm already. I'm all for a pad-bath when we get back."

"Not a bad idea," Peli said, suddenly noticing how oily she felt. After a moment, she asked tentatively, "Professor? Does Du'er have the authority to . . . to hand out statues and artifacts this way? I'm not doing anything that would sully our name, am I, in taking this with me?"

"Since Du'er is in charge of all the sculpture unearthed at this site, you're perfectly safe, my girl. Don't fret yourself."

Peli let out a breath in relief.

"You worry too much," Edisse said, a sparkle of fond humor in his green-brown eyes, "This assignment is going to be perfectly dull. It's why I chose it for your internship. Excitement should be reserved for senior xenoanthropologists."

"Oh!" Peli exclaimed, "I don't find this dull at all!"

"Somehow, I'm not surprised."

They reached their tent and parted ways; after a pad bath, lunch, and two cups of water, Peli rolled onto her bed to check her mail. The usual assortment was waiting for her: a bank statement, notifying her of the deposit of her stipend as an assistant to Dr. Edisse . . . a reminder from her dentist that her ten-year re-enamelling was due next month . . . junk mail, asking her to buy the newest fragrance from Arras Windfall and the latest technology in room decor . . . and a surprising and enchanting viseo-letter from her big sister. Doni's tales about her adventures in First Voice had always thrilled Peli as an adolescent and had been responsible for her decision to take advantage of the rich cultural fabric the Alliance offered.

No doubt Doni had some new escapade to regale her with in this letter; being a linguist on a courier ship with six people of radically different heritage never failed to create any amount of delicious and amusing anecdotes, and like every Seersa born Doni could spin a story.

Delighted at this unexpected pleasure, Peli spent the afternoon with her mail before returning to her work, refreshed. She placed the figurine on her work desk where it occupied the corner of her eye and set to translation.

"So you have reason to believe this figurine is actually related to the myth?"

"I think so," Peli replied earnestly, dipping her sweetbread in the honey pot that occupied the midpoint between herself and Edisse. "The story, if I'm following it correctly, says that Edera'yn gives Seyela a jeweled string as a symbol of his love, and that Seyela brings it to the next festival in Heaven, where she does a dance with it. This enflames Taleyira into hatred, from which I have to assume that she's Edera'yn's mate, otherwise it wouldn't have made her so angry. That's where I stopped for the night, though."

Edisse lifted a brow. "This must be hard for you. You're getting so little of the story for so much of your work?"

Peli flicked her tail, "Well, the 'plot', if you would, is pretty slow to unravel. Whomever is responsible for writing or for setting this myth down gets wrapped up in small and sometimes . . . well . . . sordid details."

"Is that so?" Edisse said with a chuckle, "Typical.

The Aera are such sensualists. They'll make poetry about anything tactile, from the silky smoothness of a certain fabric to the oily slickness of their own sweat."

"There are a few lingual anomalies," Peli continued, wrinkling her nose to Edisse's amusement, "Like this *'ruje'aida'*. 'String' is the closest thing I can find, but I know it's not quite right, but the Archives don't have a clear definition for *ruje'aida* in this time-period. It could be 'string' . . . it could be 'rope' . . . it could be 'bracelet' or 'glue'."

The old Asanii's brows rose, "Unusual to have such ambiguity in the Archives."

"If there's ambiguity in the Archives," Peli replied, driven to defend her race's efforts, "It's at least partially the fault of the race from whom the ambiguity stemmed from. We can only record what they tell us, after all."

"True, true . . . so will you go down to the digs to tell Du'er and Dr. La'aina?"

"Not yet. I want to have something more concrete to tell them. I'll probably spend the rest of this morning and afternoon working."

"Don't forget. . . ."

"I know, the party tonight." Peli watched the Asanii dip the last of his sweet-bread in the honey, cradling her tea. "How formal is this again?"

"Very. I'm going to have to wear a tuxedo."

Peli wrinkled her nose. "Oh, no, not one of those 'black tie' events?"

Edisse chuckled. "Unfortunately, yes. They've become popular again in the scientific circles these past few years. I suppose it's only fair since we regularly impose our balls and cultural affairs on them."

Peli refilled his cup. "I'd like to go to Earth someday. There's so much history there. It's like a mini-Alliance, all on one globe! Can you imagine having so many disparate cultures develop on one world?"

"Rather amazing, isn't it?" Edisse agreed, "Well, one step at a time. But if I have anything to say about it, you'll get there."

"You'll come with me, won't you, professor?"

Edisse was rolling up their breakfast mat, "Oh no, Peli-pupil . . . I have my ambitions as well, you know."

"You do?" The idea had never occurred to her, "Where would you like to go?"

The old Asanii's hazel eyes twinkled, like the sparks that betrayed the presence of a consuming fire. "To the Chatcaavan Empire."

Peli's mouth dropped open. "Dr. Edisse! You're not serious, are you? The Chatcaava, with their feudal lords and Slave Queens and subterfuge and who knows what other unsavory customs?"

"A society of shape-changers, my girl! Think of it! What kind of world would you live in if your identity was so malleable?"

"Wouldn't you be in danger?" she asked, black eyes wide.

Edisse laughed easily, "They've signed a non-aggression pact . . . which is to say, 'yes, very probably.' But you overlook the fact that life is full of perils, and that any assignment you take, no matter how mundane it may seem, has the potential for disaster. After a while in the profession, you develop a sixth sense for keeping yourself out of trouble."

"I hope so," Peli said, pushing herself to her feet, "Because you'll need it if you head into that territory."

"You should worry more for yourself . . . you're the neophyte."

"I do worry for myself," Peli replied, muzzle curving into a smile, "When I have the time between myths!"

The morning passed, lazy hours strolling after their preceding fellows with all the urgency of a cat sunning itself in summer; Peli hardly noticed when lunch-time came, barely breaking concentration long enough to bolt down a piece of tana fruit and drink more water. The story in the strips was getting interesting; Taleyira had challenged Seyela to the Rite of Defiance for laying premature claim to Edera'yn. The Seersa tagged 'Rite of Defiance' in her transcript on the data tablet for later research — perhaps it was a custom that still existed, or maybe more information was available in a historical text.

The bleep of the programmed alarm in the tablet jarred her out of her trance, irritating her. Parties! What did parties have to do with being a xenoanthropologist? Didn't those other scientists have enough to do without manufacturing excuses to do something else? Exasperated, Peli folded the strips in their hide bundle and checked her makeshift clothes rack, thumbing through all the light shifts until she found the one evening gown she owned.

Five years ago ambassadorial parties, high-society functions and balls had swept back into fashion with such fervor some historians had immediately proclaimed the renaissance of the Romantic Era. Sheath dresses returned to haute couture, exemplified by models like Silhouette, the mysterious Tam-illee with her slender, lily-like figure . . . leaving all the digitigrade races, and especially the stockier ones like the Seersa and their sister-race the Karaka'A in dismay. The beauty of sheath dresses laid in the elegant straight line they made of a figure, one impossible to create with thighs jutting out at impossible-to-hide angles.

The dismay lasted until a prominently known Karaka'An Fleet Captain arrived at a function held by Ambassador Jaimetharrl Darksoot in a sheath dress slit all the way up the skirt to her hips on both sides to al-low her to walk freely. Since then, slit-sheathes for digi-tigrade races had become the rage, and even the planti-grade females took to slitting their dresses for novelty. Peli had bought her dress at the time, never expecting to need it.

The Seersa shrugged out of her work tunic, stepped on the pad to have all the dirt and excess oil dissipated from her body, and then settled to brush out her fur. With a toe she turned the mirror to face her where she sat in front of the work table; a fruitful search of the u-banks unearthed a step-by-step viseo on how to pull up her hair with only a few hairpin-stasis fields. Peli went about her preparation as she did her work: profession-ally and without devoting much conscious thought to the results.

After pulling her hair and cheek ruffs into a french twist, the Seersa slipped on the dress; it was midnight blue, limning her torso to her hips where it fell in two straight panels, one before, one behind. The plain, high neckline lay hidden beneath a loop of dark blue chiffon, clipped at the shoulders with small silver ovals with the ends left free to trail behind her.

Peli was studying her reflection critically when the bells outside jingled. With a lack of self-consciousness born of naivete, she called in flawless Aeran, "Enter, an' the winds be right."

The tent-flap pushed back to admit Du'er, who halted in the entrance as if struck. "Could this be the same beauty I once professed an insolent desire to carve? Surely the Greater Master will strike me down for my impertinence, for I see she is already a living work of art!"

"You're not . . . ," Peli began, and Du'er laughed.

"No, I'm not lying. I promised, didn't I?" The male Aera walked into the tent; he was not yet dressed for the event or perhaps wasn't going, still sporting one of the wraps the Aera liked to clip around their hips with ostentacious jewels, male or female. "No, I came to give you a gift, and I am pleased now because I didn't know how perfect it would be! By the way, that color truly becomes you."

Perplexed at the concept of a color making her look particularly nice, Peli glanced down at her midriff. "I like it," she offered tentatively in response, then continued on the other course, "But . . . another gift?"

"Ah, but the figurine was only temporary! This is a more permanent gift. And here it is!" Du'er snapped his wrist from behind his back, opening his fingers to reveal the carefully coiled length of a thick crimson ribbon with raised geometric patterns. When Peli made no move to take it, he came to her side and gently turned her to face the mirror, artfully tying it into a bow around her right wrist. "There. It is only proper for ladies to wear gloves at evening parties, but Aren is too hot for such a custom, don't you think? This will make you look as if you're wearing gloves that had bows at their edges for effect. No one will notice you're not wearing white gloves until they truly look at your hands . . . which are, by the way, quite beautiful."

Peli stared at herself, eyes wide — if that was the effect the ribbon was supposed to have it was totally lost on her. But if Du'er said so, and he had admitted to being a poetic soul . . . besides, she'd promised not to reject his gifts.

"Thank you, Du'er. It's very pretty."

"Not as pretty as the one who graces it," the male replied smoothly, "I will see you soon."

"Certainly," Peli said, although she was in truth not very certain at all; at least, not about her feelings concerning the odd behavior of the sculptor.

"Peli? Who was that?" Edisse stepped through the partition, wearing his black and white suit and straightening his bowtie with all the absent discomfort of someone who hadn't tested the starching of his collar since its last use.

"Du'er . . . to give me this." She displayed the ribbon for her mentor, who studied it curiously.

"It's very nice. Makes you look like you're wearing gloves."

Peli blinked, then shook her head in amazement. "Really, sir?"

"You look fine, my girl. Shall we? We don't want to be late."

"Of course not."

The sun had fallen when they stepped outside the tent. Peli fell in alongside Dr. Edisse, ears swiveled forward; even from here, she could hear the faint strains of music, an effervescent piece for a string quartet she recognized as the work of a popular Hinichi composer. The occasional chirp of Aren's night insects added a curious counterpoint to the melody.

"Will we hear Aeran music?" she asked.

"I don't suppose it. The Aera aren't inclined toward background music."

". . . not even for parties?" Peli asked.

Edisse regarded her, and his fond amusement did not succeed in hiding the sober set of his lips. "They may look somewhat like us, more like us than Terrans, or Eldritch, or Sirelanders, but I don't think it's really struck you that they are *different*, despite that exterior."

"I . . . I guess not," Peli said, "but, professor, you taught that we must always start from a common ground, looking for common ground, when we work among other races."

"Of course. When working among other races, start from a common ground, look for a common ground . . . and never forget it may not be there. You must always be aware, hyper-aware, of the differences. Only then can you compensate and plan for them."

The wind tickled softly at Peli's exposed neck; unaccustomed to the sensation, she hugged herself. The faraway song had drawn nearer and mutated into a Tamleyan ballad punctuated by the hum of conversation. A magenta tent splashed with shadows of dark violet shading to black proved responsible for the noise, spreading its bulk across an area that would have encompassed six tents the size of the one she shared with the elder Asanii. Silhouettes haloed in the orangy-lilac glow of interior light sources milled across the cut-out stage of the long horizontal plane of the tent's side.

Edisse walked to the front of the tent, where the flap was pegged closed with the tassel that indicated a desire for privacy but an invitation for others to enter without announcing themselves. "Ready, Peli-pupil?"

The Seersa lifted her chin and squared her shoulders. "Ready, sir."

The Asanii unlooped the closure and let the flap drop open, stepping inside. Peli followed with some trepidation.

The tent held all of the archeologists working the nearby dig as well as all of the members of the village of outworld-scientists where they were staying, along with what the Seersa guessed were some ancillary Aera, perhaps friends of the diggers or the scientists. A trestle table occupied one length of the tent near the entrance, piled with trays of fruit, steaming meat, soups and broths, several kinds of breads, and more bowls of drink than she had ever seen collected in one place. The music emanated from a player esconsed beneath the table. Slender metal holders that rose to her chin displayed floating glow-bulbs, casting everything in a warm, amber light at odds with the walls of the tent. Beyond the immediate gathering, a large space had been cleared for dancing, along with a table for panel discussions.

Dazed by the people, scents, and sounds, Peli trailed behind Edisse as her mentor made his way through the throng, shaking hands, making greeting gestures, offering palms or waving tails, switching from culture to culture with the ease of long practice. He introduced her to everyone he met; Peli tried to keep track of the names, but after the fifth introduction the dazzling colors and scales and fur patterns merged into an endless stream of indistinguishable information. It relieved her, however, to be among the scientists, with all the multiculturalism and cheerful camaraderie that typified most of the crowds occupying Selnor where she'd gone to school. Peli hadn't realized how much she'd missed that intermingling until now.

The Seersa stopped at the food table, taking a slice of the potato bread and spreading it with white honey. A matronly Harat-Shar lynxine poured her some of the nerisii punch and Peli stepped away to enjoy a little food in her corner, trying to clear her mind of the afterimages of countless males in suits and females in formal-wear that varied from the rustling silks of the Asanii to the near-nakedness of the Sirelander's metal armor.

"This . . . this is your natural setting! You shine like a sublime jewel amid the ostentation of the gaudy would-be beauties, Terran peacocks to your subtle swan." Du'er slipped around her from behind, bowing; in the stark black and white of a tuxedo he looked the last monochrome still in an almost-completed colorized film.

He was insane, Peli thought. She was about as at home in a party as a plant in outer space, and the whole bit about the swan. . . . "Good evening, Du'er. You look striking."

The male pressed his hand to his heart and rolled his eyes in exaggerated pleasure. "Lady, you wound me with your affections! I shall never heal!"

Peli resisted the urge to ask him if he was always this theatrical. What if that was a societal custom? He would probably be offended. She cast about for a topic of conversation and managed to find one. "I've discovered a possible link between the figurine and the stone strips."

"Do tell!" Du'er exclaimed.

She recounted what she knew of the tale of the two goddesses and Edera'yn. As she finished, inspiration struck, "Du'er, do you happen to know what '*ruje'aida*' is?"

"Ah . . . a slang in Clan Roseyan and Zuene'a! They use it for the word 'ribbon'."

"That makes more sense," Peli said, tapping the underside of her chin, brows furrowed. "Although I wonder how that meaning wasn't recorded in the Archives on Seersana."

Du'er chuckled, a sly twinkle in his eye. "We must keep some secrets from you, mustn't we? Or else we wouldn't be a mystery." He winked at her and melted back into the crowd.

Peli shook her head and steeled herself for more mingling among strangers. She had to be sociable; she had to bring good words to Edisse's name. Shoulders squared, the Seersa re-entered the chaos and worked her way slowly through the tent . . . chatting with a Phoenix and admiring his metallic plumage, silently marvel-

ing over the furlessness of the one human on the science
team, discussing different kinds of pelt-brushes with a
Tam-illee, speculating with a Hinichi over the probability
of finding more intelligent life in the new sector on the
spinward border of the Neighborhood . . . Peli's mind began to swim. An hour and a half later, she was exhausted
and ready to put herself and her overworked jaws to bed.
She looked for and found her mentor by the lazy swing
of his ruddy tail.

"Dr. Edisse, I'm going to go back to the tent."

"Sleepy already?" he asked, eyes sparkling.

Peli considered, then replied with the candor that
words demanded, "Not sleepy . . . tired, tired of small talk
and smiling and trying to say the right things. I'd like to
relax before bed, do a little more of the translation."

"I'll see you later, then, if you're still awake."

She nodded and threaded her way through the people to the tent flap. The Seersa began to open it when
some sixth sense warned her of a stare that was applying
for a transmutation into a drill; someone's gaze was boring into the center of her back. Peli glanced about swiftly,
surprised, and found herself meeting the hostile stare of
the Aera female she identified after a few moments as
Dr. La'aina. Dr. La'aina? The one in charge of the dig?
What had she done to earn the wrath of that female?

Peli frowned and stepped out of the tent. She'd ask
Edisse tomorrow.

Sunlight tinted by the tent walls fell on her face the
following morning as Peli yawned, stretching in her bed-

roll. After the party she'd had enough energy only to change into her light night shift, loose her hair and then drop among her pillows. She didn't even remember falling asleep. So much for her plans to continue reading the story of Seyela and Taleyira! She would have to make up for lost time today.

Swiveling an ear towards the partition revealed no sound; Edisse must still be sleeping. If memory served, she'd heard something in her sleep; he must have returned in the dark hours of the morning. Well, she'd save a little time and eat breakfast while reading her mail. That would give her an extra half hour to spend translating.

After a cursory morning ablution, Peli set the pot of tea to warming and unwrapped some bread, plucking her data tablet off the table. She shuffled through her messages: a letter from her mother with an attached viseo from the local news about her old primary school . . . a notification that one of her many favorite authors had produced a new work, and would she like to buy it and in which format? (Terran perfect-bound? Faulfenzair scrolls? Privacy-coded file?) . . . a challenge to a duel . . . the latest issue of Scientific Explorations in Language . . . *challenge to a duel?*

Eyes widening, Peli spread that message. Her screen filled with a formal looking document written in Aeran, challenging Peli to a Rite of Defiance over the Heart Du'er, to be settled tomorrow at sun's zenith . . .

And issued by Dr. La'aina.

It had to be some sort of joke. The rest of her mail forgotten, Peli jammed a piece of bread into her mouth for breakfast, changed hastily into a more appropriate shift, pocketed her data tablet and headed into the morning sunlight. She'd straighten this out before Edisse woke up; what would her teacher say, to find out she'd somehow managed to run afoul of this culture without even trying? Hadn't he said this would be a dull assignment? What had gone wrong? It had to be a simple misunderstanding. She'd fix it. She *had* to.

Peli trotted to the dig site where most of the archeologists were already at work, skirting the colorful tents; as an afterthought she flicked on the recorder on the data tablet in her pocket, as Edisse had always taught her not to waste an opportunity. After all, the Seersa thought ruefully, for all she knew, she'd never be allowed into this settlement again. She came to a breathless halt in front of the dig-master's dwelling and grabbed the hand bells outside, giving them a rough jangle.

"Come, if the winds are in your favor," a cold voice intoned.

Wearing the knowledge of her innocence as armor, Peli walked inside.

Her first impression was of fire: red walls, bright orange and yellow pillows, hot colors everywhere. La'aina stood in the center of the tent, back turned to the entrance; in this setting, the brown of the other's pelt seemed to be a-flame, forming a halo of palpable anger. Peli opened her mouth to greet her, but the Aera female turned, saw her and interrupted.

"So it's you! You thought I wouldn't do it, that I would spare you because you're an out-worlder and should know better, didn't you? Didn't you think I would call for the Rite after what you've done?"

Faced with those raging eyes, Peli backed a step involuntarily, hand to her chest. "I . . . what . . . what *did* I do?"

"Oh! Play the innocent with me, will you, little foxy? I know better . . . I've heard all Du'er's graphic accounts of your nights together!"

"Night . . . nights together?"

"Your nights together in bed! Having little Seersa-sex! Teaching him little Seersa love-secrets! Showing off that perfectly white pelt Du'er bragged you were hiding under all that clothing! Did you think I wouldn't call the Rite after hearing so many details about your spotless, sexy white undersides?"

Peli's mouth dropped open in complete and total shock. Not only was this worse than she had expected, it was beyond her ability to comprehend. Du'er . . . Du'er had told his mate these gross and hideous lies? Why? And how could La'aina have believed him!

"Dr. La'aina, please allow me to ex—"

"Explain! Explain! You can explain it to me tomorrow when I have a pike aimed at your heart! Now get out!"

Peli complied with haste; it was obvious that trying to convince La'aina was fruitless anyway. She would have to get to the heart of the matter—the 'Heart' of the matter! With some exasperation she remembered that she had been planning to research the Rite of Defiance. She had anticipated learning more about it, but not this way!

The Seersa jogged to the small tent where Du'er had given her the figurine, anger and bewilderment lending her energy. She didn't even bother to ring the bells to request entrance, or to check the tassels on the tent-flap to make sure she was allowed to come in; flipping the cord aside, she stood in the entrance and folded her arms.

Du'er glanced up; he had been sitting on a pillow and sipping something, studying a tablet. Seeing her, he put aside the tablet and cup and stood, arms open. "Ah, it is the beauteous Peli, come to give me her rosettes as promised!"

She ignored him and interjected, "Du'er, what is the meaning of these, these unforgivable untruths you've been feeding to Dr. La'aina? She wants to kill me now!"

A flare of eager interest spurted into Du'er's eyes. "She challenged you to the Rite?"

"Yes! And she's quite intent on putting a sharp object through my midriff! Du'er, why did you tell her we were . . . were bedding together?"

Du'er leaned back, his entire body slack with satisfaction. When he spoke, his voice held mockery and amused superiority. "Because I hate her, and wanted to get away from her."

Peli choked in the middle of her next tirade. What came out of her mouth after that stranglement was a tiny, meek sound. "Why . . . how. . . ."

"You see," Du'er poured a cup of tea and offered it to her with laughing eyes, "if I could manipulate La'aina into declaring a Rite of Defiance on you, she would lose it . . . lose it because you are more knowledgeable in language than she is and would defeat her in the Verbal Challenge, and she is growing old and slow with anger and I am confident you would be able to tire her into defeat in the Physical Challenge. You would win me but wouldn't want me, and would set me free. However, if somehow La'aina did win, she'd be so disgusted with me she'd also set me free. She would never tolerate a mate she knew had been unfaithful. So you see, either way, I'd win."

Peli stared at Du'er. If she had been unable to comprehend La'aina, it was nothing to how little she could comprehend Du'er. "On purpose . . . all those things you told me, all the times you were with me . . . the ribbon!" Her eyes flew open.

The male laughed in delight, "You understand, then! Yes, the ribbon still has the same connotations for us today as it did in older days. Males give them to females they favor for display. And you, unknowing, went to a party with every single person of any repute in the vicinity wearing my ribbon on your wrist. Every Aera there left talking about it. I thought La'aina would burst. It was absolutely beautiful!"

"You were lying to me. You promised not to lie to me, just as I promised not to. . . ."

"Not to reject any gifts from me, yes," he agreed, grinning.

Peli felt like sitting down but couldn't command her knees. "You were planning it . . . even then?"

"Of course. You were the most likely candidate. You were exotic, young, beautiful and intelligent . . . La'aina knows how much I like those qualities. She wouldn't believe me falling for another Aera, but for a strange and uniquely beautiful alien? That she would swallow eagerly. All those graphic descriptions of your naked body!" He laughed, "You should have seen her face!"

"You never intended to keep your promise, then," she managed, eyes glazing.

Du'er leaned into his pillow, resting his head in the joined fingers of his hands as he stretched. "Actually, I did keep my promise. I never lied to you. I do think you're beautiful. I do think you would make a fabulous carving. I would like to be that sculptor one day. I simply omitted my motives."

Anger pushed through the fog clouding her mind, an anger completely Seersan. Peli clenched her hands into fists and glared at Du'er. "The purpose of words is clear communication. To impart information. Lying is deception, a perversion of words to fool other people into believing your version of reality. What you did is exactly the same, except you used silence instead of words! You *deceived* me! Purposefully, for your own ends! You violated the spirit if not the letter of your promise!"

Du'er chuckled, completely at ease. "I thought you would feel more comfortable with me violating spirits and silences instead of words and letters. That is what you Seersa worship, isn't it? Aren't you grateful?"

Peli stared at Du'er, open-mouthed. His laugh jolted her into action. "You are despicable!" she hissed, enunciating each word clearly, then turned stiffly and exited the tent.

The morning sunlight caressed her brow as she stood outside, trying to banish her anger long enough to think. What to do? She had been manipulated into this position so cunningly she could see no way out. La'aina was in no condition to believe her; she didn't trust Du'er *or* Peli, and nothing the Seersa could do would make her think otherwise. But she couldn't get involved in this. Not only would it make a horrendous mark against her on her record, but she doubted she would survive a physical duel unscathed. Perhaps she was young, as Du'er had so off-handedly stated, but the Seersa had no experience at all in weaponry or combat other than rudimentary training in self-defense.

What could she do?

She had no choice. She had to talk to Edisse. He would help her find a solution; he had to. But as Peli walked back to her tent, ears flat and tail hanging, she found herself fervently wishing there was some other way. Her professor would be so disappointed in her.

The scent of rooderberry-filled donuts punctuated the air when Peli entered her tent; the smell mingled with that of mint hot chocolate reminded her of the tiny piece of cold bread and the excessive stomach acid that she'd been using as fuel so far. Her mouth started watering.

"Ah, there you are!" Edisse smiled, fatigue-marks lining his eyes despite his cheerful smile, "You young people. I don't know how you can stay up so late and wake up so early. Your dedication to this project is admirable, my—"

"Sir . . . ," she couldn't stand to hear it, ears drooping. She dropped into her usual space across from him and tried to find the words.

"Oh, something's bothering you, I see. Here, have a donut and relax. You look like you need a little pampering."

Peli watched in mute misery as the old Asanii pushed a donut and a cup of minty hot cocoa in her hands. The last thing she deserved right now was pampering or praise for her dedication.

"Now," Edisse said, leaning back, "tell me your troubles."

"Sir, I've been challenged to a Rite of Defiance!" Peli blurted.

The Asanii stared at her for several seconds, then said, "Pardon?"

Peli's shoulders slumped dejectedly, "I didn't mean it to happen, but Du'er . . . Du'er manipulated me. He wanted to get away from his mate, and set it up so Dr. La'aina thought he was being unfaithful to her with me, and she believed him, and now she wants me to show up tomorrow at noon so she can kill me!"

Edisse took a deep sip of his cup before continuing. "You're certain this isn't a joke."

"Oh no! I talked to them both this morning. It's deadly earnest." Peli looked at him, pleadingly. "Isn't there something we can do? Some loophole? I never intended something like this to happen!"

Rustily, Edisse began to laugh. "I know you didn't, my girl. I never intended it myself either, come to that. I thought this would be a safe assignment! As for loopholes . . . well, let's start looking. Should we begin with the document she sent you?"

Peli nodded, "I have it right here. In fact, I left it on the screen. . . ." She plucked her data tablet from her pocket and handed it to Edisse, who studied it. A puzzled frown grew on his face.

"What is it?" she asked.

"This doesn't look much like a challenge statement. It seems to be a record of a conversation."

"A . . . what?" Peli asked, incredulous.

Edisse handed the tablet back to her, and the Seersa scanned it swiftly, then again in shock. A squeak of surprise escaped her. "Professor! This is the conversation I had with Du'er half an hour ago! I . . . of course! I left the tablet on record when I entered the settlement!" She suppressed the urge to crow with delight, scrolling through the text of both her exchanges, that with La'aina and that with Du'er. "Oh, Dr. Edisse! It's where he was admitting to me everything he was doing!"

"Well!" the Asanii said, examining it as she handed it back to him, "that's an uncanny piece of luck!"

Peli glanced up at him. "You don't suppose . . . that if I gave this to La'aina, she might believe me and call the Rite off?"

Edisse considered. "I'm not sure. Aera can be very moody. One minute they might be as stubborn as rocks, the next as changeable as the wind. It's worth a try, particularly since I suspect it's our only chance. But! Let's finish breakfast, go over the texts on this Rite, and see if we have any other options. If not, we'll go with this."

Ignoring her apprehension with difficulty, Peli managed a smile and began to eat.

Two hours later, they had discovered no loophole; if La'aina did not call off the Rite herself, there was no way to prevent it. Not only that, but no Champion had ever called off a Rite in the history of the custom.

They would have to show her the transcript.

Tablet in hand, Peli stepped out of the tent and began

the walk back to the dig for the second time that day. The sun was especially strong, the colors of the tents when she approached particularly vibrant; the Seersa felt as if everything on Aren had chosen to assault her.

Ringing the bells outside the female's tent and receiving a cold invitation to enter, Peli again strode into the abode of the predator, who was sitting on a pillow reading a report.

"You again?" La'aina bristled when she glanced up.

"Stop!" Peli said, injecting as much command into her appeal as possible without disrespect, "Listen to me! Du'er has manipulated us both!"

"I am not interested in your excuses!"

The Seersa continued, ignoring her racing heart and La'aina's stormy gaze. "He wanted to break away from you and arranged it so that you would Challenge me, and either of us would set him free if we won! He was doing it all on purpose! He was lying to you! And to me!"

La'aina glowered. "You really expect me to believe you?"

"You don't have to—I have proof! I accidentally recorded the conversation I had with Du'er where he admitted all of this! You only have to read it to see that he's been planning this all along. We were set up!"

"That sort of data can be forged," La'aina replied coldly.

Peli felt her body tensing. "Do you want to take the chance? If I'm right, Du'er will have tricked you, made a fool of you by using you like a puppet to execute his whims. Do you want to be the butt of every joke in this community? You will be, once Du'er gets away from you and starts gloating! Read the transcript!"

"I'm not interested," La'aina said again, beginning to shift against her pillow in growing anger.

"Do you want to reward him for playing you like a musical instrument?"

"*I'm not interested!*" La'aina roared, leaping to her feet, "Take your immutable tablet and get your 'sexy white pelt' out of my tent!"

"I'm going," Peli replied, fighting the urge to cringe and run, "But I'm leaving this here. Read it! Don't let Du'er get away with this! It's your name at stake!"

"*OUT!*" La'aina bellowed, and Peli gave in and ran, tossing the tablet with its incriminating evidence onto a pillow before exiting.

Outside, Peli tried to decide if that had gone well or not. What if La'aina did not read the tablet? What if it was all lost? Glancing at the workers who occasionally gave her inquisitive and sometimes knowing looks, Peli felt exasperation for Aren and its intractable inhabitants. Slipping her hand into her now-empty pockets, the Seersa walked back toward the scientific settlement through the sun and sandy terrain, ruminating on the chance that La'aina would see sense and the chilling possibility that she wouldn't. The verbal half of the Rite she might be able to handle, since all it seemed to entail was a solid knowledge of the Aeran language, its common insults and colloquialisms; as a Seersa, she had grasped those things naturally. But the physical half . . . she'd read about the weapons, and if La'aina's earlier threat was an indication of her chosen weapon, then it would be pikes: pikes that were two and a half feet longer than she was tall. Peli sincerely doubted she'd be able to keep the thing upright, much less defend herself with it.

"Any luck?" Edisse asked as she entered the tent.

"I don't know," Peli answered with a sigh, "I left it with her, but I don't know if she'll read it."

"Well, then, all we can do is wait," Edisse said, "If she chooses to retract the challenge, a courier will arrive on our doorstep. If not. . . ."

"If not, I hope we'll have a first aid kit handy for when she dismembers me tomorrow at noon," Peli replied morosely, dropping onto a pillow.

"Let's not engage in wild speculations, Miss Argentson," the old Asanii said with a slight smile, "Besides, I doubt a first aid kit will be much help in putting you back together after La'aina's finished with you."

"You cheer me so much," Peli muttered, and Edisse chuckled, patting her on the shoulder.

"It'll be fine, Pelipenele. You'll see. Now, keep yourself busy. I'll stop you for dinner."

Peli nodded and dragged herself to her desk where the stone strips lay bundled beside a borrowed data tablet. She had no heart for her work, even less when she looked at the statue of Seyela. She'd wrapped the red ribbon from the party around its base. Diabolical Du'er! How could he scheme so with the minds and hearts of innocent people?

With a sigh, Peli set to work and, as always, became lost in it. Taleyira, hot with anger, had challenged Seyela to a Rite of Defiance over the Heart Edera'yn. All the gods and goddesses of the major pantheon attended, Laera and Zleayron, Tasenear, Yesier, Aura, and Zenoa, with Luer the Peace-Father serving as the arbiter. After three days, Seyela won the verbal half of the Rite, and after a day's rest she and Taleyira met again for the physical match. As the current mate and thus the Champion of the Heart, Taleyira chose the weapons for the duel, long, curving knives.

Peli was deeply engaged in translating the blow-by-blow account of the physical duel when Edisse tapped her on the shoulder for dinner. They ate in silence; La'aina had not sent a courier, and it was growing late. The Seersa's apprehension began to solidify into cold fear, while part of her screamed the absurdity of her situation. She wanted nothing to do with any of this! She didn't want to have to risk her life to win Du'er . . . win him! She didn't even want him! How in the name of the Four Sisters had she gotten into this mess?

After dinner, Peli used her borrowed data tablet to read her mail, tail restlessly twitching against her pillows. She found an ad from her favorite orchestra on Selnor for their next performance in two weeks (she might be able to attend, if she was still in one piece) . . . a 3deo-clipping of a strange Terran musical production called Cats, sent to her by a friend who found the images of humans dressed up like Asanii very amusing . . . the latest catalog from Pathways, a company that sold reproductions of cultural artifacts . . . the news viseo from her home on Selnor. Peli clutched the data tablet to her breast and experienced a fleeting moment of true despair. She had no desire to die! There was still too much to do!

The Seersa took herself firmly in hand. La'aina would see reason and cancel the Rite. Or if she didn't, she would

survive. The Rite usually ended when an opponent yield-
ed, not with their death. There was no need to become so
overwrought.

Peli returned to her translation, but the gory account
of the physical rite reminded her of the coming event
and made her queasy besides, until she firmly abstracted
the myth. This Rite had happened in the beginning of
Aeran time, when the goddesses fought the duels to the
death as a matter of course. It was a fantasy. It had nothing to do with her.

Peli found she was a difficult person to convince.

Hours later, Edisse said reluctantly, "Go to bed, my
girl. You'll need your sleep." The rest of the statement
hung ominously in the air: when you fight La'aina tomorrow. "I'll keep a watch."

Unwillingly, Peli nodded and wrapped up the stone
strips. She turned out the light, changed, and went to
bed . . . but she didn't sleep. When Edisse's light darkened several hours later, the Seersa was still awake. And
the courier did not come.

This is crazy! This is absolutely crazy!

"This is crazy," Edisse said, echoing her thoughts.

Peli stood at the edge of the circle drawn in the sandy
earth as other Aera found seats on the nearby ground to
watch. La'aina had not called off the Rite, and in fact had
decided the physical duel would precede the verbal; as
Peli had worriedly suspected, the Aera had chosen pikes
as the weapon. The Seersa was nearing desperation: now
that the day was here and the sun was teetering at the

edge of zenith, she could feel the jaws of the trap Du'er had set closing around her.

The setting was the essence of simplicity. Near the digs, a circle twenty feet in diameter had been drawn in the earth and marked at the four compass points with stakes and tiny white flags. One tent housed the Heart and another the Champion, while small awnings had been erected to shade spectators, of which there were already a formidable number. What better entertainment than half-naked females screaming insults or trying to gut each another?

"Dr. Edisse!" she exclaimed, but couldn't bring herself to say the rest: *Get me out of this! Find a way! Help me!*

The old Asanii squeezed her shoulder and said, "Don't lose hope. There may still be a peaceful end to this."

"A peaceful end!" Peli squeaked.

"That brain of yours is formidable, Peli-pupil, or I never would have chosen you as an intern. Don't disconnect it prematurely."

The jangling of hundreds of bells announced Du'er as he stepped from his tent surrounded by seven males with rings of bells and tambourines. Forming an honor guard, they escorted him to a special awning just beyond the north end of the circle. Peli watched him with disgust, outraged by the saucy, knowing wink he awarded her as he passed her by.

With trepidation, Peli turned her gaze to the tent of the Champion. Five females assembled outside the tent and began ringing their bells. With a last squeeze on the shoulder, Edisse left her standing on the edge of the circle and sat nearby.

La'aina stepped forth amid the cacophony; she had shed all her clothing save a turquoise loin wrap that echoed the eye-burning swirls of turquoise and fluorescent teal she'd painted across her red-brown and orange pelt. Her white chest hair cascaded down to her stomach like a furry breast-plate, and she held her chin high, flashing blue eyes looking down on everything with disdain and rage. The sun set the gold of her heavy hoop earrings a-fire.

She looked a lot like Peli's mental image of Taleyira, the Warrior Wife-goddess. Too much like her.

La'aina stepped into the circle and held up her hands. The jangling stopped. "I, La'aina of Clan Sereon have declared the Rite of Defiance on Pelipenele Argentson for wearing the ribbon of my Heart's favor. I have chosen the physical duel as the first half of the Rite, and the weapon of decision is the curved pike."

On cue, an Aera stepped up to each of them, holding the six and a half foot-long staves topped with the curving metal heads and their angry spikes. The staves had been crafted of precious wood, oiled to a fine sheen. Peli glanced at her pike in horror as La'aina continued.

"As according to ritual, the Challenger may now speak words on her role in the Rite." La'aina leveled her glare on the Seersa.

Peli stared at some undefined point in the distance. Last night in bed she had rifled through hundreds of responses to this question, her only chance to speak in her defense before the slaughter began. There had to be something she could say to prevent this debacle, some way to take advantage of this last chance to speak, to make language the true weapon of this Rite, but nothing had occurred to her then. She had to find something to say now . . . there had to be something she could do!

The Aera stared at her as she remained silent. Peli glanced at her feet, mind blank despite all her frantic efforts. She wore no shoes and had chosen the lightest, shortest tunic she owned for today, sleeveless and sky blue, unwilling to have her actions hampered by long skirts or slippery soles. Already the hot sun pulled the oils from her fur, and she'd be panting soon. Something to say, there must be something. . . . Peli put her hand to her heart, hoping for inspiration.

And gasped.

"Dr. La'aina," she began, back straightening, "you have called this Rite because of Du'er's reports to you of our 'relationship' together, correct?"

"Yes," La'aina hissed, eyes thinning. Dialogues were allowed in this last statement before the duel, but they were uncommon.

"You have read the transcript I provided you with of Du'er admitting he was attempting to manipulate us, correct?"

The crowd gasped, and Du'er's face contorted into a frown.

"Yes," La'aina answered.

"And you chose not to believe it?"

"It could have been forged," La'aina said, folding her arms.

The crowd listened, enrapt, no doubt wondering what Peli was planning. Well, let them hear, then!

"Du'er did tell you on numerous occasions of our

'time' together, did he not?"

"Yes."

The sun poured on her, and Peli resisted her need to pant. There would be time enough for that later. "And he gave you graphic descriptions of my body, didn't he?"

"Yes." La'aina scowled.

"Did he tell you anything about particular parts of my body that were exceptional?"

La'aina's anger returned full-force to her eyes and body language; having to discuss her mate's glowing reports of his lover's body in front of a crowd of two-score Aera did not please her in the least. *Just a few more words*, Peli thought pleadingly to La'aina, *just a few more words and we'll expose him for what he is, and you can back out gracefully!*

"He said that the areas you hid under your clothing were as white as snow, unmarred by spot or color."

It was a reasonable assumption, Peli knew. Her rosettes spotted only the gray areas of her fur on the many parts of her body exposed by her summer clothes. Du'er the sculptor, the visual artist, would certainly have observed that. "He mentioned no exceptions, no spots at all?"

Du'er looked worried, the crowd excited.

La'aina frowned, more in puzzlement than anger. "No."

Peli caught her fingers in the lacing of her tunic and pulled the neckline down, exposing the one, perfect rosette an inch and a half beneath her left collarbone. "He didn't tell you about this one, then . . . because he's never seen it! He was lying to you, Dr. La'aina!"

The crowd roared. Du'er leaped to his feet in dismay as La'aina stared in shock at the rosette, not even the size of her open palm, the rosette that gave lie to the words of the Heart.

"He wants to leave you, La'aina," Peli finished calmly, heart pounding beneath her chest and hands trembling as they held the lapels of the tunic apart.

The female turned her burning gaze on Du'er and slowly grinned. It was not a pleasant expression. "Then he won't get the chance." She held up her hands, "I am calling off this Rite! It is . . . unnecessary."

The crowd laughed and cheered, breaking away from under the awnings to surround La'aina. Peli didn't notice; she slowly sank to the ground, mouth open and tongue lolling, heart drumming a frenetic staccato. She'd done it!

"I want the ribbon back," La'aina added to Peli, almost an afterthought.

"I'll return it immediately," the Seersa promised fervently.

The honor guard that had escorted Du'er in was now escorting him out, some of them angry, others amused, and still others with expressions of pity. As they passed her, Du'er managed to jostle them to a halt and stared down at her, eyes cold with wrath.

"You never mentioned that rosette," he hissed.

Peli smiled thinly and answered, "You never mentioned the meaning of that ribbon."

Du'er would have spit on her had his comrades not grinned and dragged him away, leaving her with Edisse, who had pushed his way through the crowd to her side.

"Told you, m'girl," he said affectionately.

Peli groaned. "Where's that first aid kit? I think my heart's going to explode."

"I think he already did," Edisse replied with dancing eyes, watching Du'er's receding back.

Two weeks later, Peli leaned on the wall of her bunk on the courier ship *Truewind*. Her small bag was packed securely above her in the luggage compartment, while a carefully cushioned box formed her foot-rest. Pillows formed a nice back-rest for her, *proper* pillows that she'd found on her bed, not serving as furniture on the floor. She was reading her mail.

'The Edera'yn myths, translated by Pelipenele Argentson, form a substantial and fascinating body of previously unknown mythology from the Aeran culture. Edera'yn, the Fool-Lover god, apparently occupied the unique status in Aeran mythos of comic-relief.'

"Are you reading that article *again*?" Edisse said, leaning on the doorframe with folded arms and a grin.

"Well . . . yes," Peli replied, "It's the first time I've ever been in a journal!"

Edisse laughed, "I know, I know. I was the one who saw it first, remember?"

"Only because they send professionals copies of the journal first!"

The Asanii chuckled and said, "Well, you're on your way to professional status yourself. Your handling of the incident on Aren was masterful."

"Thank you," Peli replied smugly. She shifted her feet

on the box.

"You never did tell me what that was," Edisse said, pointing at her foot-rest.

"Just a gift," Peli answered easily, "A token souvenir from Aren."

"Ah! Well, get your rest, Peli-pupil. We'll only be on Selnor for three days, then it's off to Phoenix-Nest."

"Yes, sir!"

Peli watched her professor leave. Her eyes fell on the box, where the figurine of Seyela and the ribbon nestled in the packing material. She grinned.

'Edera'yn's adventures trying to romance every goddess in the pantheon and the resulting mischief add a whole new facet to our understanding of the Aera. Hitherto, we had never seen instances in their tales of an appreciation of the ridiculous.'

Peli leaned back and laughed in glee, exhilarated. If her assignment on Aren had been intended to be 'dull', well . . . bring on the rosettes and ribbons!

The Elements
of Freedom

"**B**UT I'M NOT AN ambassador," Carevei protested, her hands on the edge of the desk flexing as she stared at the wallscreen. "I don't even know these people, or anything about them!"

"We sent an ambassador. He didn't do much good," the tired human male in charge of the ad-Ciracaa Embassy replied. "Maybe if we send a scientist instead, they'll listen."

"But why me?"

"You're the one who discovered the fault line." One of his pepper-gray brows rose. "Do you want those people to die?"

Carevei's muscles tightened through her back. "Of course not."

"Then go out there and convince them to get the blinding fire off that piece of land before it's too late. They'll listen to you, EarthHunger. You know what you're talking about."

Her ears flicked back against her skull. Carevei closed

her topaz-colored eyes and said, "All right." She heard the chime that signaled the connection's close, and tilted her face slightly to the right; the warmth of Ciracaa's brilliant yellow sun painted the inside of her eyelids red, touched her lips and drew the moisture from them. She turned away to pack.

Sixty-two hours later, the Tam-illee foxine leaned against the window of the dragonfly and watched the endless gold plains rush past. She'd taken the assignment to Ciracaa after four years of wandering Tam-ley, frightened of the path that had beckoned her. Her intention had been to become a chemist, but halfway through her schooling an errant elective on seismology had seized her attention so tightly she'd been unable to resist the inevitable change of curriculum. Her father would have called it flightiness, had he known. Carevei herself didn't understand what about the breaking of the earth attracted her so, but three years later she'd emerged from school a seismologist on a planet with few earthquakes and several hundred thousand fellow earth scientists.

The university-sponsored job on Ciracaa, then, could have leaped out of a dream. It still seemed like one after seven months. The Ciracaana had proscribed high technology across most of their homeworld in an effort to preserve their ancient culture; only in the Twins, the two starport cities on either hemisphere, could off-worlders and natives alike partake of the Alliance's vast technological harvest. Carevei lived in Nguva, the northern city, but it was the wilderness that drew her—the broad oceans rimmed with pale lilac sands, the low blue mountains streaked with silver-gray, and above all, the endless

plains of sun-bleached grasses, hiding beneath their velvet nap the corrugated, secret heart of a violent earth.

In all the months she'd spent on Ciracaa, Carevei had
met few natives, and all of them in the city. As the dragonfly drew her ever closer to her drop-off point, she felt
a moment's cold doubt—that she would fail to convince
the tribe living there to move, that it would be destroyed
by the earthquakes she'd predicted would begin as soon
as a month from now, that somehow, her having discovered the fault would make her responsible for any lives it
claimed. The Tam-illee splayed her hand against the glass
of the window and let her temple rest against it.

"Stop!"

Carevei stiffened where she crouched in the high
grasses. Her dusty taupe fur would have been perfect
camouflage had she not had a head of hair the color of
a panther's back. Moving silently through shifting grass
wasn't one of her most practiced skills anyway, and she
had absolutely no desire to disobey such an aggressive
voice.

"Stand up . . . slowly!"

She rose, inch by painful inch, above the ears of wild
grain.

Twenty feet away, a barbed spear as long as she was
tall traced a circle like a reticule over her distant rib-cage.
A ripple of amazement traveled her body at the sight
of the Ciracaana warrior who held it; the civilization
cradled to the breasts of the city natives had obviously
never touched him. He was a tower of wiry muscle at al-

most ten feet tall, his lower half the supple four-footed body of a brown feline with splotches of gray, white, and black, his upper half a bare-chested foxine biped's, complete with a thin demi-muzzle and black-backed triangular ears. His golden hair fell braided over one shoulder, wrapped with scarlet leather cords; gold armbands flashed from his biceps as he moved, and a crude but ingenious harness around his lower barrel and second chest supported a number of variably-sized pouches.

The phosphorescent blue eyes, accented with whorls of white and crimson paint, had fixed on her with the intensity of a laser. She felt oddly overdressed. "Do you under the protection of another tribe travel?"

Carevei repeated the ritual phrase from her Embassy reading session. "I travel alone. I am a Starfallen."

He lowered his spear, and she gradually deduced from the tension of his ears and mouth that he scowled. "Another off-worlder. Have you come your disgraced cousin-member to retrieve?"

"I have come to speak with your Sun Mother," Carevei replied.

His mottled tail lashed once, disturbing the grass around his lithe body. "You have come to us to lie as your cousin-member has?"

"I have come to speak with your Sun Mother," Carevei said again, beginning to tremble and ignoring it to continue firmly, "My words are for her, not for you."

His hiss startled her so much she jumped backwards before she realized he was laughing. "You do not know what you walk into, Starfallen, but you may the path you have chosen follow, good or ill. I will to the camp of the

Lifehawk escort you."

"Thank you," Carevei said. The words shook only a little.

An hour through folds of grass-felted earth proved long enough for her escort to deposit her on the edge of the camp. He vanished before she could thank him, leaving her disturbed at how quietly he had moved. Turning her gaze back to the path before her, Carevei cast aside her seven-month-old innocence and looked for the first time at the seasonal camp of a tribe of the Ciracaana. A score of octagonal hide tents was arranged haphazardly in a cleared-away space; their painted sides fluttered in a faint breeze, glistening with images of birds and animals in ocher yellow, clay red, mineral green. Eight-sided designs of rocks outside and to the right of each tent's entrance resolved with further observation into deep, small firepits.

The Tam-illee hesitantly walked into the cleared area, detecting no signs of habitation until she became aware of the rustling of feet and the low murmur of words, contrasting strangely against the city-dialect she'd learned. Beyond a cluster of tents, she stumbled onto a round area bordered on almost all sides by grasses higher than her waist, and there—bodies, movement, tension. Thirty-odd of the natives, their hides striped and spotted every color from white and pale rose to slate blue and black, sat restlessly in a rough circle around a solid female of their race and a biped male who was not. Carevei moved forward, sandy ears rotating towards them.

"It is for the off-worlder time to leave," said a ruddy male with geometric patterns painted in white across his second back. "Of his talk we have enough heard! He has no words to us to say."

Low, angry murmurs rose at this comment, to which the off-worlder in question, a wolfine Hinichi, said wearily, "I've told you the truth again and again. If you won't listen to reason, then you will have to listen sooner or later to reality."

Carevei's ears folded back. Ambassador or not, even she could be more tactful. She stopped a few lengths away from the circle and called, "He's telling the truth."

Thirty-odd faces whipped to face her, braids flying, spears digging into the ground. The sudden object of their attention clenched her taupe-colored hands and said, "My name is Carevei EarthHunger. I'm a seismologist from Nguva. I discovered the fault your camp is sitting on."

"Another Starfallen," someone muttered.

"You must move to where it's safe," Carevei said. "This place will not fit that criterion very soon."

"Those are the words of the other off-worlder," a young female said. She stepped out of the circle to look at the Tam-illee, her green eyes a shock of color against the black-striped white of her pelt. "Why have you been sent the same words to say?"

"Because no one wants to see you hurt," Carevei answered. She grasped her courage steadily in hand and strode to the circle's edge, facing the female in the center, the one decorated in paint and medallions that splintered the sunlight into the shapes of hawks and deer. "Are you the Sun Mother?"

"You address her."

Carevei bowed from the waist. "Sun Mother, the danger is real. I am a scientist. It is my job to know such things. Please, move to a different camp this season."

"Are you willing yourself to prove?" the female said. Beside her, the Hinichi male frowned, tail freezing in exasperation.

Taken aback, Carevei answered, "Of course."

"You are willing then, to undergo the rite your tribe-cousin would not?"

Her stomach seized into a knot. "What . . . rite do you speak of, Sun Mother?"

The Ciracaana stared down at her. "The rite of the Vessel. You will seek of a totem its approval, and become of its wisdom a receptacle. Only then can we of your truth be certain."

Carevei glanced around at the inscrutable faces, then at the sullen ambassador. "Is that the only way you'll listen to me?"

"Yes," was the implacable reply.

The Tam-illee foxine bowed again, feeling the sun on her back through the thin fabric of her white blouse. "Then I will do it."

The circle erupted into cacophony, the Sun Mother's strident voice reigning over it. "Ylriasna, take to the tent the Starfallen and prepare her! I will the bones of the elements make ready."

Carevei found a white hand encircling her upper arm as the striped female who had spoken earlier answered, "Yes, Elder!" and began to direct her out of the furor. Once around the corner, the Ciracaana said, "Come! I will in a tent place you, and help you make ready." A spark of excitement edged her words.

"Ah . . . thank you, Yl . . .Ylriasna?" Carevei worked her mouth around the name, ears falling at her poor pronunciation.

Ylriasna only hissed in what the Tam-illee took to be a giggle, leading her toward a large octagonal tent near the outskirts whose taut sides displayed leaping grass-cats in titanium white. "Do not be worried. I find peculiar your name, as much as you do mine. What did you say it was?"

"Carevei EarthHunger."

"Is that your tribe's name?"

Carevei shook her head, dark hair moving over her shoulders. Her blouse was already streaked with sweat. "It's what my people call a Foundname. When you discover something that has changed you completely, you name yourself after it."

"And why did this name you choose? EarthHunger?"

A chill coruscated across Carevei's spine. "I'm not sure. It's what I chose to do. I learn the earth." Knowing how little of an explanation it was, she said, "I hope I haven't offended your tribe as my . . . cousin-member . . . did."

Ylriasna pulled open the flap. "Do not over your conduct be worried. You've already this camp pleased with your willingness to do what your cousin-member would not."

"I see," Carevei said, wishing she did. She walked into the tent, aware that the far taller Ciracaana was ducking to follow her. Inside, a hammock stretched diagonally from the center pole to two of the eight shafts forming the outer perimeter. The interior was far larger than she would have imagined smaller biped nomads building. Several blankets of tanned animal hide had been meticulously folded to display the geometric designs dyed on them to best effect. A small wicker chest sat against the wall nearest the entrance, and most incredibly, a lamp hung above it, glowing a pale green that provided a soothing illumination for a tent whose deep shadows seemed inappropriate to the summer afternoon outside. The Tam-illee walked to the contrivance, touched her fingers to its base. Octagons of real wood formed the top and bottom, and between them a skin thin unto translucence provided the light's egress.

"How does it work?" Carevei asked, her fingertips gently probing the edges. She heard Ylriasna sit behind her.

"The light-cages? We put in them worms with some food. In the dark, they glow."

"Amazing," Carevei murmured. She stared at the lamp. "You really made these? The wood . . . where did it come from?"

"It did not from the sky fall," was the bemused reply. "We for the wood trade with the tribe of the Longfoot. The worms live in wood longer." Ylriasna folded her arms. "Why are you with the light-cage so fascinated? It is a simple thing."

"But it's not," Carevei murmured, surprised at her own interest. She shook her head, trying to define the emotion and failed; she said again, "It's not."

Ylriasna studied her for a few moments, then said, "Come, Starfallen. About the Vessel's Rite I must speak and to this telling you should listen closely. Would you like to sit?"

She realized abruptly that she would very much like to sit. Carevei lowered herself to the ground and folded her legs beneath herself, resting the sides of her wrists on her knees. She trained her gaze on the Ciracaana, observing briefly the almost flawless verticality of the stark stripes that girded Ylriasna's lower and upper body, even in her mane. Zebra, she thought suddenly. Terran zebra.

"The important thing in this rite for you to seek is the approval of the totem," Ylriasna said earnestly, leaning forward. "You will know that this you have gained when you are given of his visitation a tangible sign."

"Like what?" Carevei asked.

"Like a feather. Or the hairs of a tail, or a broken tooth," said the Ciracaana. "Something to us you can bring back to show."

Surprised, Carevei said uneasily, "Then I'm supposed to actually see one of these animals?" She'd detected none of the local fauna while walking through the grasses toward the village.

"Just so," Ylriasna answered. She smiled, a distinctive combination of dipped ears and wrinkled nose that Carevei had seen once or twice in passing on the faces of the city-natives. "If you with such a sign return, then you will have in the tribe status enough to be listened to."

"There's no more? I just walk out into the prairie, wait for an animal to pass by, pick up some of its sheddings, and come back, and you'll move?" The Tam-illee steadied herself with a hand on the ground. Why had the Hinichi ambassador not agreed to so simple a process?"

Ylriasna shifted; uncomfortably, the vixen thought. "No. The totem must to you speak. You must have the visions. That is why I must prepare you with the paint, and why the Sun Mother is for you crushing the bones of the elements."

"The bones of the elements," Carevei repeated uncertainly.

"Yes. The leavings of the eight elements. Wind, sky, fire, sun, stars, moon, water, and earth. When we administer the bones to you, to your success at having visions it will add much."

"Drug!" Carevei exclaimed. "You're talking about a drug!"

"I have heard your cousin-member call it so," Ylriasna said. She raised herself on her four, supple feline legs. "But we are time-wasting. The totem you are seeking must choose you, and then we can begin painting."

Carevei's tail flicked. "I have to choose one? That makes it harder."

Ylriasna shook her head, and Carevei could just detect something like amusement and curiosity in the other's mannerisms as the Ciracaana opened the wicker chest and reverently lifted from within it a large black satchel. "Starfallen! So strange you are! Mere people cannot a totem choose, as if the symbols of life were theirs to command. The totem will choose, not backwards. Now," she sat before Carevei and stretched open the little mouth of the satchel, "put into the bag of the void your hand, and let the totem guide you."

Carevei studied the Ciracaana's face for a few heartbeats, seeing in it a sobriety that leaped past the boundaries of an alien body language, and turned her attention to the satchel. No light penetrated its depths, no hints allowed to what she would find within. Silently, the Tam-illee vixen slipped her hand into the bag. Fingertips met cool metal, thin discs sliding over and over one another. She grasped one, trying to discern its shape by feeling its edges. When an unexpectedly sharp corner sliced open one of her fingers, she could not quite throttle her gasp.

"That one! Take it out!" Ylriasna sounded much older, as if channeling a wisdom deeper than her experience.

Reluctantly, Carevei withdrew her prize and held it up for the Ciracaana to see. The shape of a bird of prey, symmetrical wings outstretched on either side of a head in proud profile to the right, reflected all of the light of the lamp—save on the edge of its spread tail where the Tam-illee's blood stained it.

Ylriasna stared with green eyes as wide as stones. "The lifehawk, the tribe totem. And it has marked you already. This is a powerful sign." The Ciracaana looked at her, face still slack with astonishment. "I do not who you are know, Starfallen, but the elements can in a way touch you that I have not of another off-worlder heard. It is mete that the Sun-Mother wants you to succeed."

"She does?" Carevei asked, startled. That the tribe's elder had emotions seemed improbable.

Ylriasna wrinkled her nose in a definite grin as she replaced the satchel in the chest and lifted out a dizzying array of baked clay jars, each marked with a bright color on its lid and walls. "If she did not, she would not to the best ritual painter in the tribe have sent you. Undress, and begin we will."

Reassured and belatedly aware that her tension was a combination of anxiety and excitement, Carevei pulled off her blouse.

Seven hours later, Carevei stood naked before the Ciracaana of the tribe of the Lifehawk, naked despite the short white shift clasped at her ribcage with a band of incised gold, despite the dagger on her leg ritually tied in the ceremonial knot of willingly relinquished power, despite the heavy armbands and masses of jewelry, bells, bracelets, earrings. Spending the hours in silence with only the soft susurrus of Ylriasna's breathing and the occasional plangent sound of droplets of falling paint had eased her into a fugue as flowers and leaves and abstract animals and designs grew out from her spine. The movement of the brush had stripped her of the years she'd taken her body for just a part of her, forcing her awareness of each limb, each hair, the groove of her hips, the rise of her buttocks, the slope of a shoulder blade, the swell of her biceps. Standing in the flickering shadows of the torches ringing the meeting circle, Carevei felt herself a newborn, her senses tingling in every square inch of her pelt, her skin as she stood in the vespertine dark.

The Sun Mother stepped forward, a young female beside her cupping a clay bowl so brilliant a white shadows proved incapable of clinging to its surface.

"Carevei of the tribe of the Starfallen off-worlders. Have you been by a totem chosen?"

The Tam-illee lifted her chin, hearing the soft plaint of the bells woven into her night-dark hair. "I have,

Elder."

"Let now these others hear your claim."

Carevei took a deep breath, then lifted her hand to touch the stained medallion centered over her forehead. She recited the formula Ylriasna had taught her. "Lifehawk chose me, Lifehawk claimed me, Lifehawk has by blood already marked me."

Soft murmurs ran around the edge of the circle. Carevei could just detect the slight widening of one of the Sun Mother's eyes.

"Carevei EarthHunger Starfallen. We have your claim heard. Upon your return with the physical mark of the lifehawk, we will know for truth your words. But the elements to court is a task difficult for those of us who for the joy of earth forsook their symbolic life. Help we will offer you. Are you for the bones of the elements prepared?"

"I am," Carevei answered.

"Then receive this gift, and be to the elements abstracted." The Sun Mother gestured for her handmaiden to come forward and lifted from the bowl a slender reed. She leaned forward, grasped Carevei's chin firmly, and tipped her head back.

"For wind."

The Tam-illee closed her eyes, felt the mild summer breeze against her exposed upper back and legs, controlled her jolt of surprise as the Ciracaana Elder blew a short, sharp puff of dust up her right nostril. A chill ran like water down her back. She could hear the breathing of all the thirty-odd Ciracaana watching her, felt their gazes on her.

"For sky. For fire. For sun." The reed slid out of her right nostril and into her left. "For stars. For moon. For water. For earth."

The warmth of the Sun Mother's hand against her chin dissipated. Carevei let her head down gently, her hyperawareness extending past her body into the air where the night seemed to saturate its molecules, painting them black. The Tam-illee focused with difficulty on the Ciracaana Elder.

"Now we bind your eyes and to the sacred place take you, there to succeed or fail as truth will judge."

Carevei felt the dark fabric shutting out her eyesight, almost moaned in protest as the sense that had grounded the abnormal amount of information seeping in through her ears, her skin, her nose vanished, leaving her nauseated and disoriented. Her arms lifted; she thought it was of their own volition, but the tingle at the tips of her fingers whispered songs to her of someone else's hands, grasping hers firmly, drawing her forward. The Tam-illee clove through the night, as if each needle of hair on her body had become a knife to pierce the thickness of the air.

The walk drew out interminably, a thread of minutes faintly connected through the haze of her perception. The vertigo she experienced came, not as a result of sudden motion, but of its sudden halt.

"May you by the elements be guided," the Sun Mother said, the sash unwinding from around Carevei's head. She blinked open her eyes and saw no one, the Ciracaana all melted away into the shadow-spikes of the grasses in the moonlight.

Carevei EarthHunger stood alone on the prairie, her face lifted to the breeze falling like a benison from the sky. No city lights drew attention away from the stars; no sounds interrupted the melodies of wind on grass. The pressure of the lifehawk medallion against her forehead soothed her fear and doubt, and she lifted her arms to the swollen moon, her breathing deepening, the bells in her hair and tail tinkling.

"Lifehawk . . . ," the words leaped from her mouth, her palms outstretched, fingers curved to cup the pale light, "Lifehawk, if it is your will to save these people, grant me your visions!"

Her ankle snapped as the earth lurched beneath her and slammed her down. Carevei gasped past watering eyes, digging her nails into the soil as the ground bucked, the bells in her hair jangling. Earthquakes? It was too soon! The results of the tests hadn't predicted any activity until the plates had moved for another month! The Tam-illee's eyes widened. The tribe! She had to get to the tribe, to warn them, to tell them to leave, it was too soon, something was wrong, wrong, wrong . . .

Wrong . . .

The thunder of the earth ripping apart, so familiar, forgotten. The wooden walls around her begin to collapse as she clutched her stuffed gryphon to her chest, too petrified to move toward—

Toward the beams beginning to crumple.

Toward the screams of shattering crystal.

Toward the figure holding out a hand, the bemused astonishment frozen on her face as the ceiling buried her, her, her . . .

Mother!

Carevei screamed against the ground as it snarled and shuddered. "Mother! Dam-ley, Mother! No. . . ." She sobbed, turning her face into the soil. "It ate my mother. The earth took my mother from me. Oh, Iley, Iley, Iley . . ." The words rushed out of her as inexorably as the memory, crashing through a wall as old as her childhood. She tilted her head back as the anguish seized her, and in her defiance cried, "NO!"

A screech higher than hers made her throw her arms in the air, ducking away from the bloated face of the moon. Feather-edged patterns blocked out the light, and her nose filled with a spicy-sweet scent reminiscent of the bones of the elements. She felt something ripping at her, and instead of flailing, she became utterly still, stretched like an archer's bow with her arms an arc to the sky.

Her arm trembled beneath the weight of a hawk, mantling its wings as its talons sank into the top of her right hand. Carevei's tears dried as it folded its wings, staring at her with pale gold eyes that matched her own. Her grief drifted slowly into a pool at the center of her body.

"Lifehawk," Carevei whispered.

Shifting on her hand, the hawk stared away from her. Blood dripped into the nest of torn grasses threshed by her convulsions. Carevei quivered under his weight, physical and not. It returned its gaze to her, eyes far more alien than any Ciracaana's; she saw herself reflected against those gold surfaces, broken from a battle she hadn't even known she'd been fighting all of her life. She saw the peace beginning to settle in her face, and the surprise that she'd hadn't felt it in so long.

Talons gripped her hand, tearing across tendon and bone. The hawk lifted its wings, feathers spreading, and vaulted from its living perch, circling up into the sky. Carevei watched it, trembling, teeth chattering with the shock, until against the disc of the moon she saw no smudge.

The hyperawareness rushed back to her. The blood curling around the edge of her hand to fall to the ground set her nerve endings afire. The sensuous friction of the broken bones of her ankle lifted the hair all along her back. Sweat darkened her pelt and soaked through her hair, slicking against the medallions and jewels there, but the familiar pressure of the lifehawk medallion against her forehead gave her strength. Carevei rolled onto her hands and knees and, gingerly and with determination, crawled in a direction she sensed would lead her back. Compared to the journey she'd just finished, a few hours through the grass of Ciracaa, even mangled as she was, seemed simple.

"Are you sure you felt nothing two nights ago?" Carevei asked again.

The black-striped Ciracaana shook her head. "It was of your visions a part, Kar-e-vey."

"I was so certain . . . ," the Tam-illee shook her head, shifting where she rested on a packed sled to rearrange her reset ankle. The silence that deepened between them had nothing of discomfort, and so Carevei let it sit until her companion broke it.

"What will you do now?" Ylriasna asked.

Carevei carefully refolded her arms, favoring the bandaged hand that had given the Ciracaana the physical sign they'd needed to believe her warnings. The bustle of the packing tribe soothed her, and she watched as another tent, deprived of its center pole, deflated like a popped balloon. "I don't know. I suppose I'll go back to my work."

"You do not enthused sound," said the Ciracaana.

"I guess I'm not," Carevei admitted after a few minutes. She tipped her head towards the sky, eyes closed against the brilliance of the nooning sun.

"Now that you have identified the spirit that drove you, and discovered your own it wasn't, you have no energy for the study of the earth's hunger," Ylriasna said.

The Tam-illee froze, eyes half-opening. "Yes. That's . . . that's it." She shook her head. "But it's what I've done all my life. What is there to do now?"

"Stay with us," Ylriasna said. "We will new ways teach you." Carevei saw her shock reflected in Ylriasna's eyes as the Ciracaana paused, then said, "Are there not in the Starfallen tribe those who make of their lives the study of others? You could 'study' us. We would welcome you . . . the tribe totem gave you a vision such as has not been seen since the time of the heroine Menagliia. If it has freedom given you, should you not leave the cage?"

Carevei stared around her with different eyes. A child capered past, graceful despite the lower body he had not yet grown into, playing chase with one of the older children charged with care-taking. Two Ciracaana pulled down one of the larger octagonal tents, its painted sides glistening cobalt blue. The sun limned the edges of their bright jewelry, just as it filtered through the tall grasses and gilded them.

Her fingers traced for her eyes the bird of prey incised into the gold band around her upper arm, but they felt the satin of the wooden bottom of the light-cage. She thought of the dozens of medallions in the bag of the void, each made by some craftsman by a method she could not conceive of, wondered who had discovered the bones of the elements and how the rite of the Vessel had been constructed around it, thought suddenly of all the things there were to learn above the hidden earth.

"If . . . Lifehawk will have me," Carevei said, not quite believing the words even as they left her mouth.

"Lifehawk already does," Ylriasna said, her entire muzzle disappearing the one vast wrinkle, a grin the size of her face.

"Then . . . I'll stay," Carevei, realizing as she said it that it was her desire above ought else.

"Hei-la! I will the Sun Mother tell right now, that Lifehawk's chosen will with us remain, that Carevei EarthHunger is of the tribe now!"

"No," Carevei said suddenly.

Ylriasna stopped, mid-leap. "No?"

"No," the Tam-illee said, feeling the taste of her liberation even as she answered. "Not Carevei EarthHunger anymore. Carevei HawkFreed."

Ylriasna's face wrinkled into a grin. "It is mete." The Ciracaana turned and darted through the commotion toward the center of the camp, toward the tribe Elder. Carevei watched her go, then lifted her face to the sun.

PANTHEON

TWO YOUNG HARAT-SHARIIN women lay on their bellies on the carpet; one a striped tigraine with loose chestnut-hair and a tail that had a tendency to curl during concentration, the other a spotted cheetahine, narrow-hipped and long-limbed like so many of her intrarace. On the carpet between them lay a spread of colorful cards: winged catlike women in pale robes, fierce nude griffins all golden with loincloths of lake and gemstones, sinuous hexapedal half-ghost creatures in blue and rime-white.

Spotted Renya watched, ears trembling, as her best friend reached for the deck lying between them. The next cards would mean the difference between victory and defeat. Five years of playing, honing her skills as she planned her way off-world permanently, had not rubbed the shine off this final moment when she discovered whether she'd won.

We made a deal, she reminded Kajentarel and the Angels, *I play to please you. I win. I get a ship . . . you get an altar. Remember!*

Her friend paused. "You sure you want to play this last round blind?"

"Yes," Renya said. She set down her card. "Go ahead."

Dani matched the card with one of her own, then flipped over the Condition card.

Laughter fluttered Renya's veil, laughter tinged with relief and the headiness of success. "My Iley wins over your Naem-fili!"

Dani sniffed, ears flipping back in good-natured frustration as she touched the face of her card. There was no doubting the outcome: the Condition card read, 'Sense of Humor,' and on her card the avatar of the Malarai, the Naem-fili, was depicted as teary-eyed, while Renya's god of the Tam-illee had a most definite smirk. "Stars and Angels, Renya, but you *always* win at Pantheon! What, did you bribe the gods?"

Renya grinned. "Something like that." She collected the cards and began to re-order them as her best friend stood for a stretch.

"All these years, and I've never won a game. Your life is charmed, *arii*," Dani said with a yawn as she dropped on the bed. "So, when are you leaving?"

"The shuttle takes off tomorrow morning," Renya replied, sliding the cards back into their case. They were getting old; she was looking forward to the expanded set she'd ordered a few days ago. It would be fun to shuffle crisp cards again . . . particularly the ones that were coming, with their promise of novelty and adventure. "I've already packed."

"And then it's off to orbit."

"To do great deeds!"

Dani snorted, folding her striped arms behind her head. "Great deeds! *Arii*, we're smack in the middle of the Neighborhood of the Alliance. Wars and pirates are fireside stories used to frighten toothless old ones and little kits. You just wanted to join the Homeguard so that you could fly around in sleek, dangerous ships."

"True," Renya admitted with a grin and said, "All right. To avoid becoming someone's seventh wife!"

"Now that's the girl I've known since before she was old enough to don a veil," Dani said. The tigraine propped herself up on an elbow, eyes darkening as she looked at her friend. Quieter, she asked, "Will you visit?"

"If I can," Renya promised, setting her deck aside. She tucked one of her blonde tresses behind a rounded ear and took her friend's hands. "But only you. I might even take you for a ride, if I can get one of those 'sleek, dangerous ships' to myself!"

"You won't. You'll find some lionine or tigraine male you'd much rather impress!"

Renya tugged at the edge of her veil and cast her eyes up to the ceiling innocently. "Well . . ." She paused artfully. "Only if he's an officer I can bribe into giving me a permanent position."

Dani laughed and threw a pillow at her.

None of the women of the Homeguard wore veils; with teeth bared fearlessly in companionable grins, they went unfettered. It was one of the reasons Reyna had wanted so desperately to join: to walk freely, without having to demurely bat her eyelashes and avert her eyes!

Who wanted to be the umpteenth wife of a male, forced to work her way up the ladder of favor through excellence in the arts of bedding and frequent childbirth? Certainly there were Harat-Shar who didn't hold with entrainment being the most sacred mission of a female, but Renya had not grown up among them. She'd had to fight hard enough just to get the chance to go off-world, and she knew her relatives were just waiting for her to fail so they could instruct her on the proper filial duties of a daughter of an already unpopular intrarace like the cheetahine.

It was not outside the realm of the possible that they might get that chance. She had won herself a coveted place on one of the Homeguard vessels, but Renya was a just a cadet . . . not quite a nobody, but certainly not one of the crew. She could be displaced for someone more promising if she failed to distinguish herself on her first cruise.

"Do you always win at Pantheon?" her new roommate asked in disgust.

"I've played a long time," Renya said, shuffling through her cards before slipping them back into their box. She had wanted to try out the extension set that had finally arrived, but Cordasha hadn't been willing, claiming that playing with such a set was "unnatural."

"Hmph," the lynxine threw herself onto her bunk in a sulk. "I bet you couldn't beat the commander."

Renya froze, one hand caught in the act of stroking the side of the box. "The Commander plays Pantheon?"

"No one's ever beat him. I doubt you could, for all your weird luck." Cordasha wrinkled her nose (her oh-so-visible nose!), tail curling in bad humor. "He's such a difficult man. I heard this story—"

Her room-mate rambled on, but Renya barely heard the words. She stared at her old set of cards, then at the new set, the one with all the human deities. If she wanted to walk without a veil, she had to prove herself. And she couldn't lose, not with her promise to the Angels in force. . . .

"—and I still don't know what he's waiting for, I've been here three years and still haven't gone up so much as a single rank . . . Renya? Renya! Where are you going?"

She was already out the door.

Audacity was always to be commended among the Harat-Shar. Theirs was not a fleet bound together by law, rank and rigid hierarchies, but by passions and personalities. Though she did not know Commander Kerov well, Renya knew it would be better to be bold than to hope for him to notice her. A proper Harat-Shar had tooth and claw—and showed them! So she went seeking him, paying her own trepidation no mind.

She found him with the executive officer in the mess. They made an interesting contrast together, the space-black second with his sleek pate and silky hair, and the commander, a ferocious lionine whose tawny hair was almost as mane-like as one of the felines who'd contributed part of the Harat-Shariin DNA so many centuries past. Their conversation did not seem as important to her as her own need, so she marched to their table and stood beside it, shoulders straight and ears high.

They both glanced at her; with indulgence, she thought, for her interruption.

"Well, Cadet?" Kerov said at last. "What's on your mind?"

"I heard you played Pantheon, sir," Renya said, deciding to hold nothing back. The film of her veil felt especially annoying; such words deserved to be spoken without one. "I haven't lost in five years. It would be nice to play against someone who might give me a challenge."

"Five years," Kerov said, brows lifting. "Is that so."

"Yes, sir," Renya said firmly.

"And you seem to think you have the right to ask for some of my time, just so you might have the relief of a worthy opponent?" he asked.

Put that way, Renya almost quailed. But her spine stiffened. She would not, could not go back home. "It might also entertain you, sir," she said.

"I hate to tell you, Cadet, but I've long since given up Pantheon," the Commander said. "For much the same reason that you seem to be seeking new players. It's entirely too boring to win all the time."

"But sir—"

"Truly, Cadet," Kerov said, shaking his head. "There's nothing in a deck of Pantheon cards that can surprise me anymore."

"Not even a human expansion set?" Renya said recklessly.

"A what?"

The look on the executive's face was heartening; he'd gone from mild amusement to alarm at his commander's change in mien. Triumphant, Renya said, "Scores of new

cards, sir, depicting the vast number of gods and goddesses and spirits and saints of the humans. They have
far more than any of us Pelted, sir, even though they're
only one race to our many. They have so many religions
that this deck was ten years in the research and creation,
and it was only just released two weeks ago. I have one of
the first printed."

"A new deck?" the Commander said, mostly to himself. He rubbed his chin. "A new deck. I would never
have known, I stopped following the news . . . how many
cards?"

"Two hundred," Renya said.

"Two hundred new cards," Kerov murmured.

"Yes, sir," Renya said, relaxing. She grinned. "Should
I schedule the briefing room?"

"No need," the Commander said, rousing himself.
"The mess hall will do fine. Bring your cards here, Cadet."

"Right now?" she asked.

"Right now."

Renya reflected as she trotted back to her room that
sometimes she was cursed with too much success. She'd
been hoping for a private session with the Commander
so that when he lost there would be no one to witness his
embarrassment. Playing in the mess hall risked attract-
ing an audience, and then how would he behave when
she drew the winning card? But there was nothing for it.
She had thrown down the challenge, and he had accepted
and named his conditions. Her chance at a life among
the stars, among a brotherhood—and sisterhood!—of

fierce, like-minded individuals was at stake. She had to play to win.

It wasn't until she reached her room that she realized her mistake. She had promised to play with her new set . . . but she'd never burned incense to the gods of humanity to guarantee a win. She froze, all her fur standing on end.

What if she lost?

"Where are you off to now?" her room-mate asked, and seeing her with her hand on the deck. "Oh, tricked some wet-eared bastard into playing you, did you?"

Stung by the other's tone, Renya lifted her chin and said, "I am going to play the commander. And when I win, I am going to climb the ranks, and it won't take me three years either."

"Oh really?" the lynxine said, sitting up with a grin. "I bet you'll lose."

"I never lose at Pantheon," Renya said, willing it to be true, and left. As she paced the too-short path to the mess hall, she clenched her teeth. *Let me win*, she asked the human gods. *And I'll give you the same deal I made Kajentarel. Just let me do this!* And as an afterthought as she reached the mess hall, *I'll burn you the incense after this.*

"Deal the cards," the commander drawled on seeing her. Just as Renya feared, there were already a few hangers-on. She took the seat opposite him and broke out the new deck, shuffling. She offered him the deck in case he wanted to also, but he shook his head, so she dealt out five cards each and set the deities cards in the center before reaching for the condition cards and shuffling those as well.

Kerov was already studying his hand, rearranging them. Renya picked up hers and suppressed a frisson: fear? A thrill? After years of play, the gods and goddesses of her Pelted Pantheon deck were like old friends, and in this stage of play, the stage involving the most strategy, she had always known instantly whether she would be keeping all of her hand or discarding some of the cards. But these human deities . . . they were all complete mysteries. Should she keep some of them? Discard a few? She usually tried to balance her hand between male and female, well-worshipped and obscure, happy and vengeful . . . making sure she had a card to play to the most common condition cards.

"No info-film on these," Kerov said on the other side of the table.

"No, sir," Renya said, a little prim. "Money doesn't grow on trees."

"For cadets, maybe," Kerov said, grinning.

"The deck has a booklet," Renya said, pulling it out of the case. "Shall we consult it?"

"No," Kerov said. "Let's wait until the play starts." His grin acquired more teeth. "Makes it more exciting that way."

Renya almost sighed. Almost. She didn't want her veil to flutter. She examined her hand again. She had some kind of blue four-armed snaggle-toothed female; a tonsured man in brown robes surrounded by animals; a grey-eyed woman in a white gown tied in gold cords bracketed with olive trees; a man in tights with a harp and an open mouth; and a pale woman in colorful flowing robes with no less than four fox tails. She had no earthly idea what any of them stood for, but she decided at very least that she had too many women in dresses—it seemed as good a reason to discriminate as any—so she discarded the fox-tailed one and pulled another from the deck. This one was a feathered snake, and she was so puzzled by it that she decided helplessly to keep it. She wondered if Kerov was as mystified as she was and hoped so.

"Ready?" he asked after discarding two and picking two to replace them.

"Yes," Renya said, determined.

Kerov turned over the first condition card. They both leaned over it.

"'Esteemed for trickery,'" Renya read. She looked at her cards while Kerov flipped through the book to the concordance in the back. He put down one card after some reading, a dancing man with what looked like the head of a Hinichi wolfine. Renya borrowed the book to check her own cards and made a face. "I've got nothing."

Kerov grinned. "Point to me, then. This Coyote loved tricks."

Renya sniffed and said nothing as he picked two more cards to replace his winning one. Once he was done arranging them, she picked the next condition card.

Kerov said, "Historically recorded as an actual human being."

"Ha!" Renya said and paused. Now that she'd looked up her cards, she knew she had two such . . . which to play? The musician or the animal-lover? She chose the last one on a whim and put it down. "Here. St. Francis of As . . . Assisi."

Kerov frowned. "I've got nothing."

"My point," Renya said, trying not to purr. She picked two more cards: a brown-skinned man surrounded in corn and rainclouds and a woman in a black gown with crows. "Your turn to turn over the card."

Kerov picked the next condition. "Tied to the seasons."

Renya pursed her lips. Was this Chac a god of seasons for bringing the rain? Rainy season *was* a season . . . she put it down just as Kerov put down a plump woman with a basket of grain: Demeter. Looking at the rain-god's corn and his own goddess's grain, Kerov shrugged. "Looks like a draw."

Renya let out a breath. Behind her she heard several murmurs and glanced over her shoulder: the mess hall was noticeably less empty now. She suppressed a quiver of nervousness and returned to the deck.

"Your turn," Kerov reminded her.

"Right," she said. "We're tied, one point each and one draw." She turned over the next.

"Presides over battle," Kerov read.

Renya looked from the grey-eyed goddess to the one with crows. Which one? She decided on the one in the black dress—black was for death, wasn't it, most times? Kerov also put one down, a fierce-looking man in a helmet, bearing a round shield.

"Another tie," Kerov said.

"I'll break this one," Renya said. "I have two battle deities." She set down the grey-eyed goddess . . . not without some fear. Spending two cards to break a draw meant she'd win the point, but she could still only draw two cards from the deck, not four. It limited her choices going into the final rounds.

"Right," Kerov said. "Your point."

Renya pushed the cards to the side and drew her next two: a heavily-muscled blond male with a hammer and a sloe-eyed woman with a cocked hip and a knowing smile. She examined her cards, then lifted her eyes and met the Commander's across the table. He cocked a brow at her as he reached for the condition card.

"Hearth-guardian."

Renya examined her hand and shook her head. Kerov smiled and put down a friendly, round looking woman with elaborate curls: Hestia.

"That's two and two," Kerov said, drawing his two cards and pushing the last pair to one side. "Looks like our final card will decide the game for us, eh?"

"Are you having fun?" Renya asked, bold.

"I believe I am," Kerov said, grinning. And said over his shoulder, "And so is everyone else, eh?"

Their watchers—quite a few by now—cheered. Satisfied, Kerov turned back to the game. "Last card, little cadet. Care to draw it?"

"Of course," she said, squaring her shoulders. She had very few cards left, and this . . . this would be the hand that decided whether she impressed the Commander or knew disgrace.

One last card, she thought. *I just need one more point. Please, human deities! I am a good and devout and* ambitious girl, *and you will love being worshipped on my ship when I win it!*

"Preached love."

Renya set her goddess of love on the table—

—as Kerov put down another human man, in brown robes and crowned in a halo.

"Angels!" Renya said. "Not another tie?"

"Venus versus Christ," Kerov said. "Can you break this one with a second card?"

"No-o-o . . ."

"But we're tied for the win," Kerov said. "That means we draw another card and see which of our love gods fits it better. Go ahead, little cadet. Let's finish this game."

Renya pulled a condition card with fingers that trembled just a little. She cleared her throat and read, "Popular among other races."

Kerov scratched his head. "Looks like we'll need the reference look-ups."

As they took the data tablets handed them by eager crewmen, Renya reflected this was *not* how she'd imagined her winning game going. She hadn't lost yet, though. She bent to her task.

"Looks like this Christ spread to all sorts of human cultures," Kerov said after a few long minutes.

"This Venus was referenced in popular songs centuries after her formal worship ended," Renya said. "Humans even named a planet after her."

"A planet!" Kerov exclaimed. "That's hard to argue with."

But as he was talking, Renya's eyes were drawn back to his card. She kept looking at it. And then her ears sagged.

"I'm inclined to give you the win," the Commander was saying, but Renya shook her head slowly.

"No . . . no, you won," she said. She did a quick search on her data tablet and then gently set it in front of him . . . displaying the card of the Hinichi messiah from the original Pantheon deck. On it, a man in brown robes with a halo crouched before a pack of wolves. "Humans might have named a planet after Venus . . . but their Christ became the god of an entire Pelted race."

She stood up and pushed her chair in, fighting her disappointment. "Congratulations, sir."

As she turned to go, Kerov said, "Hold on there, Cadet."

Renya froze, then turned, head bowed. No doubt he would have some condescending words for her about daring to play against her betters. She hoped he would hurry it up; she could barely stand the gaze of the people in the mess hall. That they should witness her humiliation!

"This is fascinating!" Kerov said. "Most interesting game I've played in years, and with an honest player—now, now, Cadet, stop looking so woeful. Sit, deal again. Let's see what strange gods we end up with next round."

Stunned, Renya sat across from him.

"Oh, and . . ." he leaned over the tablet and plucked the veil off her. "Leave this off, I can't see your face. Now, shuffle . . . Renya, wasn't it?"

Her heart slowly lifting, Renya said, "Y-y-yesss." And grinned. It was a fine trick these human deities had played on her, giving her the spirit of what she wanted, if not the thing she actually asked for.

You've earned your statue on my ship when I get it, she thought, *along with Kajentarel's and all his angels . . . but I'm putting you on the bridge where I can keep an eye on you!*

"You going to shuffle or think all day, Cadet?"

Blowing out a breath through her very free nose, Renya grinned and took up the cards again.

TEARS

"I'M NOT CRYING," Milara said as he let her in.

Paul laughed at the habitual greeting. "I know. Come in, make yourself at home."

The human smiled as he took her wet cloak for her and hung it on the pegs on the wall, watching as the Tam-illee foxine settled herself on one of the lush velvet pillows strewn on the floor. The fire crackling in the hearth dispelled some of the darkness in his living room, but even from across the room he could see her clearly: her unusual, hairless face, the triangular ears parting the chestnut brown hair, the symmetry of her long-limbed body, and the smudges dripping from the bottom of her eyes to the middle of her cheeks, perpetual tears.

Milara let out a sigh, ears sagging as she sank into the pillow. "It's so nice to be inside. The trip here was uncomfortable."

"I imagine," the human replied. "Would you like some tea?"

"Not now, thank you." She glanced at him. "You said

you had a surprise for me?"

Paul lit a candle and brought it with him, sitting across from her on the floor. "I found a new game I thought you might enjoy."

The lack of fur made it far easier to discern her blushing. Milara averted her eyes. "Paul, you know I don't like games."

"I know. I promise this one isn't frivolous. It's a Seersan card game I found at one of the import shops." He tilted his head, watching the shadows move across her face. The discoloration on her cheeks blended with them and he suppressed a smile. "Trust me?"

The Tam-illee's naked tail twitched on the gray carpet. "Okay," she said after a moment's hesitation. "How do we play?"

Paul grinned, sliding the cards out of the box. "It's actually pretty simple, but I have to put them in order first. How was your day?"

He didn't have to watch her to know she tensed. He slipped 'The Tree' behind 'The Sojourner' and waited patiently for her to reply. In all the two years he'd known Milara, she'd never spoken favorably of her job.

"I survived it," she said finally, each word wrenched separately from behind her teeth. "If only the clerk would file his reports on time, I wouldn't have half the problems I do. Today I found a receipt from six months ago that completely messed up the totals."

Paul shook his head. "You need a new job."

"You say that every time I see you," Milara answered, tail flipping from floor to pillow in agitation.

"Yes," he said.

With an exasperated sigh, the Tam-illee stood and began to pace. Paul tucked 'The Healer' behind 'The Coat of Arms' and paused to watch. Despite the dark spaciousness of his living room she still managed to describe an invisible cage with her movements. He returned his attention to the ordering of the cards. It was far less disquieting.

Milara eventually sat back down. The air flow stilled as the apartment reached its set temperature, and the candle's flickering ceased. When Paul glanced up again, the image of her face lit by fire struck him. The lines of grayed pink that ran down her cheeks stood in stark contrast to the pale gold of her skin, and her great storm-colored eyes dominated features full of shadows, creased by frowns. A flash of lightning outside disrupted the patterns and he offered the cards to her.

"Shuffle them."

Warily, Milara began to cut the deck. "This isn't one of those mystical things, is it?"

The human shrugged. "Mystical things can only exist if you believe in them, right?"

"Right . . ."

"And you don't, do you?"

"No," Milara said, mouth firming. "None of that. No Iley, no Speaker-Singers, no messiahs, no angels, no Heaven."

"Then this isn't a mystical thing. Think of it as a psychological thing."

The Tam-illee opened her mouth to protest but he held up a hand. "Just shuffle the cards, *arii*. And when you're done, draw two of them."

The muted drumming of the rain distracted Paul. While Milara handled the cards, he turned his gaze to the wall windows. In the distance the lights of the ground-port pierced the drizzle, smeared stars fallen from the night sky. He watched them, praying that his plan would work.

It took several minutes for Milara to set the deck down and choose two of the cards. She laid them in front of her, face down on the gray carpet, and then folded her hands uncomfortably in her lap. "Okay," she said, her voice small in the darkness.

Paul put the rest of the cards away. "The game is simple," he said. He tapped the first card. "This one represents what you think you are . . . and this one," he touched the second, "is what you truly are." He watched her eyes widen. "Turn them over, *arii*."

For all her skepticism, the Tam-illee's slender, hairless hand hesitated over the first card. He could see her trembling. Steeling herself and lifting her chin, she flipped it over.

A picture of a white Seersa foxine female, her hair dissolving into a gossamer fog behind her greeted them both. Strange writings poured down the white female's back, and in one hand she held a silver bowl. A silver comb sat between her perked ears. The background behind her was painted in daubs of salted green and silver, touches of blue fading towards the edges.

"What is it?" Milara asked.

"Rispa . . . one of the Seersan Four Sisters." He touched the name on the bottom of the card. "The goddess of Ice. She is cold and unapproachable, as ephemeral as mist. Her ruling spheres are displacement and ennui."

"That's . . . what I think I am?" the Tam-illee asked, voice wavering between belligerence and apprehension.

"I don't know," Paul said, lifting a brow, "Is it?"

She didn't answer.

"Turn over the other one," the human said.

Milara rested her fingertips on the back of the second card. Her lips pressed into a thin line. She flipped it over.

Another female, this one bright orange and red with streaks of flame blue and white. She had been caught in the act of dancing, her body boldly painted in a few sinuous strokes. Behind her a galaxy whirled and white stars pooled at her feet as if drawn there by an invisible force.

Her breath shallow, Milara traced the name at the bottom of the card. "Ka . . . karesing," she pronounced tentatively. "Is that right? What does it mean?"

"That's the Dancer," Paul answered. "She holds fire within her, a fire that consumes her so totally her body is colored like it. Her joy is so intense the universe feels compelled to dance with her. Her ruling spheres are purpose and fearlessness."

"What I am," Milara said, then exclaimed, "But I don't believe it! I'm no . . . no fearless dancer."

Paul took a deep breath and stared at her. "I think you are. I can show you."

"Show me?"

"Come with me." He held out his hand, and she took it after a moment's pause. He led her to the dark bathroom. "Close your eyes. Trust me."

"Okay," she murmured. Her dark lashes fluttered

down.

For a moment, Paul simply looked at her face. When he'd befriended the Tam-illee more than one person had asked him why he'd bothered. 'Iley didn't mark her face with tears for nothing,' one had told her, 'she never smiles.' He'd discovered they were right . . . and that even when she did smile, the stains running down her cheeks made a mockery of it. During the course of their friendship, her predicament had nagged at him. Other than the peculiar birthmarks, Milara might have been born beneath a lucky star: smart, thoughtful, lovely.

But she rarely smiled.

Paul grasped the Tam-illee's chin gently in his hand and dipped the other into the pot on the sink. It had taken him months to match the color exactly. He lifted his thumb to her cheeks and gently dragged it from her lower eyelid to her mouth. The cold cream made her flinch, but she stood otherwise motionless as Paul painstakingly erased the stains beneath a layer of second-skin paint, designed to last several weeks. He massaged it until the visible evidence of the cream faded, and then looked again at his friend of two years. He bit his lip.

He guided her until she stood opposite the mirror, then said, "Okay."

Milara's eyes opened and her lips parted. She reached out to touch her reflection. Standing beside her, Paul found he could not look away.

Navigating life with the falsified evidence of tears marring one's cheeks must leave a mark. The human had known it the day he'd met her, but it had taken years to consciously realize it. Seeing the shock, the wonder in her face, he knew that she had never drawn the same conclusion.

"Aren't you the Dancer?" Paul asked.

She traced her golden cheeks and whispered, "I don't know." And then, a few moments later, "Maybe."

He folded her fingers around the pot. For a moment, she only stared at it . . . then her fingers tightened and she smiled at him.

Paul received the postcard after two weeks of silence. He spread it across his wall screen and Milara's voice filled the living room as a starscape scrolled past.

"Dear Paul — I've just arrived at Starbase Ana . . . from here I'll be leaving for Seersana and Karaka'An. I'm not sure what I'm going to do now that I've quit my job, but I'm going to take the time to find out what it is I want. You should see this place! It's beautiful. Just looking out the windows makes my heart soar. Maybe I should work on a base, or a station, or a ship. . . . but there's so much to see and do and decide first. I think I'll enjoy it here. Please send me a note if you have the time . . . I'd love to hear from you.

"Oh . . . by the way, Paul; I'm not crying.

"All my love, Milara."

Paul touched the wall screen and then his cheeks: they were wet. He laughed and wiped them before sitting to compose an answer.

BUTTERFLY

"**I** CAN'T BELIEVE FATHER'S actually gone," Geneviive murmured to her brother as their *tollies* longwalked shoulder to shoulder.

"Good riddance and Godspeed," Jared answered.

"Jared!"

The Hinichi glanced down at his sister, ears flicking back beneath their frost-guards. He could barely see her lupine face through the modesty veils the brittle summer wind snapped around her delicate face. "Oh, *decherna*, admit what is only the truth. We were a *sathet* household before Grandfather died, almost down to the last servant in the stables. It was our belief. When Father came, he only alienated people by preaching the *pruscha* sect. Dahrengard was never poured to be *pruschani*, whatever Father wanted."

"And now he's gone," Geneviive said again, ears sagging. She did not deny her brother; she never bothered when she knew he was right. "Now we are the Dahrengard-*scain*."

"Lord and lady of the Heights," Jared agreed, watching the empty wagon bobble over the uneven, frosted road. His eyes sought the shadowed streaks of the keep, black towers jutting from ragged cuts in the icy mountainside. A fitting home for the Hinichi wolfines. He licked his nose once. "Now we can set everything right."

The smaller woman started. Her voice dropped to a low hiss, barely trusting the wind to keep the words from the ears of unsuspecting relatives and servants walking before them. "Everything? Everything, Jared?"

He returned her gaze, eyes a blue somber as river stones. "Everything, *decherna*." His face turned in profile to hers, as he watched the approaching road. "I will send for her myself. It is past time."

Geneviive closed her eyes, rolling her lip between her teeth. It would not do to be seen crying when she had not wept a tear at the funeral. Instead, she held out her gloved hand and felt through the leather and fur as Jared clasped it in his. "A sister, Jared. Our sister."

He squeezed her hand.

The depths of summer had at last come to Hinichitii, and the stands of wildflowers that carpeted the lower hills of the Teeth streaked unexpected colors across the base of the mountain range: pale saffron and milky ivory, blue-violet. Jared reflected that there might even be butterflies as he scanned the brown grass on the edges of the tarmac. As children, he and Geneviive both had been entranced by those few that had braved the peaks, living flowers that danced on cold winds rife with pollen.

His sister pranced back from the control flat, still holding the bouquet of Heaven's Breath and bottlebrush she'd picked for this day. Her brown face glowed stronger than the weak sun, dark blue eyes sparkling.

"They say the shuttle just asked for clearance. It's on its way down now. No more than another twenty minutes."

"Twenty minutes," Jared mused. It had been warm enough to wear his summer's best, including the loam-brown velvet doublet he so infrequently had the opportunity to wear. "What will she be like, do you think, sister mine?"

"Oh, I hope she would be like us. She is kin," Geneviive answered, tugging her cobalt blue cloak over her shoulder as she scrutinized the sky.

"But kin that has not met us . . . or very nearly hasn't. Kin that hasn't stepped foot on Hinichitii since she was a babe too young for memories. Kin that might not even have been raised Hinichi. . . ."

"Oh, Jared! To say such things! Some things are in the blood, sure as God is in every stone," Geneviive answered, ears flipping back in dismay.

Jared chuckled softly and touched his sister's cheek. Her veil had been draped across her throat today, as was proper for a lady in the company of brethren. "Ah, *decherna*. Do you know how much I love you?"

The Hinichi turned her face far enough to kiss his unfurred palm and smiled, leaning into his hand. "Only as much as I love you, *chuniisu*."

He pulled her close enough to embrace her, but not so tightly to crush the flowers, the purr in his throat a contented rumble.

"Look, oh!" Geneviive pointed at the silver wink in a crisp powder-blue sky. "That must be her. Oh, I so hope she will like it here. Jared, tell me it will be so. My heart will break if Noelle does not love us. I know I shall love her on sight."

"Ssssh, ssh," Jared said, kissing the top of her head and releasing her. "The *tolly* can't be saddled before it's bought. We can only be our best for her, and hope she does not find us wanting."

Their hands slipped together, hers gloved against the thin chill, his naked, and brother and sister watched the shuttle descend toward the only landing strip within three hundred lopehours. Geneviive had never seen anything like the sleek Alliance shuttle; by the time she'd been old enough to leave the keep, the small Alliance embassy nexus at the base of the Teeth had been dismantled. But Jared recalled the seemings of things outside their world from his brief visit to that nexus, and the friendly concern of the human doctor who had helped him so long ago and all unknowing, had a hand in the shape of events today.

The predator-shaped shuttle slid to the ground, the reflection of the weak sunlight becoming a brilliant shield against its stylized wings. The wind's whispers carried further than the hushed thrum of its engines as it powered down. A door gaped open in its flank, and several men hopped to the ground, waiting for the ramp to fully extend. As they off-loaded luggage and crates, another portal irised apart in the shuttle's shoulder. A leggy man in leathers against the cold swung down without waiting for the stairs to fully engage. He turned to offer his hands back into the shuttle.

The sudden pain of his new signet ring catching his partially-furred finger forced Jared to realize how hard he and Geneviive squeezed against their anxiety.

The pilot backed away, lending a gentlemanly grip to the figure that appeared at the top of the stairs.

A female figure.

Her face swept across the tarmac and snagged on them. She handed something to the pilot, stepped off the shuttle, and walked directly toward them.

"My God," Geneviive whispered.

She was tall as a needle-tower, her grace evident even through the heavy tunic and breeches. The wind teased the edges of her unlined cloak around her boots. Her oval face held a human's alien beauty, but her coloring owed everything to the *Hinichisene*, for she was one of the rare wolves-of-all-seasons. The colors of her face and hands and tail flowed like liquid paint from the crisp cool of winter's white through spring's ocher and yellow-brown to summer's deep browns and finally to the gray and black of autumn. Hoarfrost-pale, her eyes only slightly recalled the blue that had bred true through Dahrengard's last six generations . . . and her hair curling around her throat contested with the snow of the highest peaks and won purer to do justice to the equally white, black-tipped Mother Mary ears, a pattern acclaimed among the Hinichi for its loveliness.

Such a picture of poise and ethereal grace was their lost sister that Geneviive did not realize until minutes later that she wore pants! and an expression of such coolness to rival ice. "My God," she said again, more in herself.

"She looks like a pagan goddess," Jared murmured.

Geneviive gasped, "Jared! God will strike you down for that tongue. How could you—"

"Look at her," Jared said, his voice low and his eyes focused on the approaching wolfine female. "Would you say her beauty is like unto a saint's? An angel's? It's too earthly for that. It's like magic. She's not of our world, Geneviive."

"She's beautiful," Geneviive said wistfully, for the frost in those pale eyes did not bode well, "And I love her, just on looking upon her, as I said I would."

The woman paused, some fifteen armslengths away.

Jared stepped forward, his hand disengaging from Geneviive's. "Hale and God touch your head."

The stranger's molasses-smooth mezzoalto seemed poorly matched to her hesitation before answering. "You called me here."

"We did," Jared said. "I am Jared, the Lord of Dahrengard, and this is Geneviive, my Lady-sister." He drew Geneviive to his side.

She studied them both, half a head taller than Geneviive and only a ear's length shorter than Jared. "I'm Noelle."

"You are our sister, and rightful co-inheritor of Dahrengard Heights," Jared said.

Noelle's ears twitched. "Me?" she asked with cool disbelief.

"You," Jared agreed.

Geneviive stepped forward and offered the bouquet.

"Noelle . . . welcome home."

The woman took the flowers only because, Jared thought, she didn't know what else to do with her hands. "I've never even heard of Dahrengard Heights."

"Then we shall make up for lost time," Geneviive said, smiling up at the taller woman. "Father did not fool with the laws of inheritance, and for us that means that the three eldest of the lord's progeny rule the land as a triad unless or until other circumstances prevent."

"What circumstances?" Noelle asked, her voice hardening.

"Like marriage into another barony," Jared offered, "Or renunciation."

"Then I renounce your . . . title. I don't know Dahrengard. I don't even know this planet. And I certainly don't know you!"

Geneviive's ears sagged and she said, "Oh, Noelle . . . please. . . ."

"And you have something worthwhile to go back to?" Jared challenged. He stepped forward and wrapped his arm around Noelle's wrist. "Do you have a home elsewhere? Family? Friends? What do you have to lose?"

Noelle bared her teeth in a ludicrously gentle human mouth. Her canines were barely pointed. "My time."

"Think of the potential benefits," Jared continued, staring down the slight distance between his eyes and his lost sister's. "You can go back to your empty hearth . . . or be a ruler of wolves here. Why make a hasty decision?"

The perfect white and black ears flipped backward, but Noelle's voice had lost some of its predatory chill. "There is wisdom in careful decision-making."

"So there is," Jared said, stepping back. Geneviive stared at him, conveying her amazement by the tilt of her ears and the cocking of one hand. He indicated something with the butt of his chin. Geneviive followed it and pursed her lips.

Noelle had not loosed the bouquet.

"Come with us," Jared said. "Come see what we might offer you."

Noelle glanced from one to the other before nodding once.

"You actually live in a castle?" Noelle asked.

Jared glanced at the wolf-of-all-seasons; she hadn't uttered a word on the ride up the Teeth, and Geneviive's wilted ears and twitching tail betrayed the strain of the silence. He waited for the gate guards to wave an arm in salute before replying, "Where else would a Hinichi live?"

Noelle's eyes darted to his face, narrowing, before she inevitably turned her face back to the heights.

Broader, larger holdings could ostensibly be found on the northern continent. In his frequent outings with his father, Jared had beheld many, yet each and every one had lacked a brutal edge, the harsh quality of line and elevation that defined every needled tower and barbed gate of Jared and Geneviive's home. The six towers that sprang from the slant of the Furrowmount had the arrogance of spears, their conical roofs blackened as if fire-hardened. The half of the fort holding built out of the mountain side sported variegated rock in black and white — winter and autumn's palette without the touch of spring or summer's warmth. Watchmen patrolled the thick walls of the battlements, where the drape of a fine net of powdered snow stressed how altitude prevailed over the season.

Seasons, Jared thought, were fleeting. The mountain snow was a truer symbol of the resolve of Dahrengard.

The gates trundled open for the three, the path leading to the keep cleared of the powdery ice. Jared took Geneviive's hand and gestured for Noelle to walk alongside. She stared at every man and woman who bowed to them as they passed.

"Do they always do that?"

"It is only proper," ventured Geneviive. "We are Dahrengard-*scain*."

"Skyne?"

"Dahrengard-*scain*," the smaller woman corrected. "Leaders can never be parted from their lands. You cannot have '*scain*' without 'Dahrengard'."

"So it means leaders?" Noelle asked, shying from a kitchen-maid who had paused to curtsey, buckets and all.

Jared said, "Or 'nobles'."

Noelle frowned, ears tilting and eyes narrowing. "Did you learn Universal for my sake? Or am I expected to learn your tongue?"

"Our tongue," Geneviive said.

"We don't have one," Jared finished. "At least, not an entire one. If the Hinichi ever had a full language, all the evidence of it we have left is a relatively sparse vocabulary."

"Pretense," Noelle muttered.

"Heritage," Jared countered, and lifted an arm as

the wardens opened the great black doors of the keep, each emblazoned with the jagged mountain sigil of the heights. "After you, *dechernasen*."

"What does that mean?" asked Noelle of Geneviive sotto voce.

"It means 'my sisters'."

Noelle's ears flicked back.

Jared stopped one of the guards passing through the anteroom. "Have Mariescha, Elijah, and Josephiat meet us in the audience chamber, please, Canton." He waved the women through the small room. "There'll be time for the two-breath tour later."

Noelle stepped away from the tapestry she'd been examining with obvious reluctance, boots thudding dully on the stone floor. "Where are we going now?"

"To the audience chamber so we can have the fealty ceremony."

The wolf-of-all-seasons stopped abruptly, her Mother Mary ears sealed to her skull and her tail a lance. "I haven't signed up for this yet, Jared. I haven't agreed!"

Geneviive worried at her sleeve, glancing from one of them to the other. The guards politely studied the wall-hangings. Jared, however, did not flit an ear-tuft.

"I know you didn't. But while you're here, I'll have you treated as you would be if you were staying. How else will you know what you're signing up for? It can be undone."

Geneviive bared her teeth at the near lie and stared at her brother with large eyes. He ignored her.

Delicate fingers the color of spring touched the flowers she'd tucked into the sash at her waist. Noelle's eyes traveled briefly over the tapestry of the *birschot* herders on the richly-colored lawns of a summer in the Throat. Her ears, tail, her shoulders all slowly bled their tension and she nodded. "You're good, Jared. If I had to have a brother, I suppose I could have had a stupider one."

Jared forestalled his sister's outraged protest with one hand on her shoulder. He smiled at Noelle and said, "I've been called shrewd. It might breed true in the family. Please, follow us."

The strange wolf-of-all-seasons could barely keep her eyes to herself as Jared led her through the narrow greeting hall and into the courtyard, where the frosted blue of the sky's bowl offered a ceiling higher than the ones even in the needle-towers. The bubble of the tumbled rock fountain sounded crisply in the clear air. The shallow pool was rimmed in gray granite, its eastern edge interrupted by a mound of rough mountain stones. Noelle crouched beside its western edge, leaning over to touch the water and hissing softly.

"It's cold!" she exclaimed.

Geneviive smiled and said, "The courtyard fountain is cooled in summer before it reaches the pipes."

"Cooled?" Noelle asked, rocking slightly on the pads of her feet. Her chin lifted as she searched the mountain back of the holding. "You have hot springs?"

Jared lifted a brow ridge. "Good guess," he said. "Taste it."

Noelle dipped her head, sniffing her fingertips with her humanoid nose. Jared rolled his bottom lip between his teeth as her tongue flicked out against her nails. For a brief instant, her face slackened into a gentle curiosity, strands of white hair sifting the small breeze that circled inside the square courtyard. She had tasted without hesitating.

"No minerals," Noelle announced, then glanced up at brother and sister. Her thin black brows with their comma-shaped marks lifted. "It's filtered? You're hiding technology."

"We live in castles, but we're not savages," Jared said gently.

Noelle studied them with her hoarfrost eyes, her face again unguarded.

Geneviive said, "The courtyard fountain is just symbolic. There are filtered springs in the kitchens and the cleaners. Our hot springs are coveted throughout the northern continent."

"I see," Noelle said, her face gradually closing. She stood, wiping her hand on her thigh. "I'm ready."

Jared captured Geneviive's hand and led them further west, to the Life's Path doors. Set into the face of the mountain, they marked the entrance to the impregnable inner holding where the Dahrengard-*scain* and their staff and closest relatives made their dens. One door had been carved of white stone, the other of black. Along the rims of the doors, two designs had been repeated as edge decorations: on the white side, a set of branching lines within a circle, and on the black side, a simple horizontal bar bisecting a circle. Jared paused before signaling the door wardens. Noelle reached out to trace the reliefs with her fingertips, the nails releasing tiny puffs of ice crystals, and the Hinichi smiled even as he noticed her propensity for touching everything.

"The Life's Path doors," said Jared, anticipating her. "The growing branches of life, the sleep of death. A reminder that before we are given the light and leisure of Heaven, we have responsibilities on this world we are not allowed to throw off."

"Nice," was Noelle's sole, wry comment, but her fingers lingered on the reliefs until the wardens rolled the great rectangular doors into their pockets.

When their ancestor Dafid Dahrengard had carved the Heights out of Furrowmount's breast, he had not been searching for a comfortable abode. With holders to retain and rivals to contest, a fort suited him better than a palace. The interior doors leading into the deepest recesses of Dahrengard opened into the audience chamber, for Baron the First had no time to spare. He had intended to impress his visitors immediately and keep them malleable to his suggestions. No addition his successors contrived could stave off the stark majesty of the chamber beyond the Life's Path doors.

Thin windows added by Masard, Baron the Fourth of Dahrengard, let in a watery light from the rafters of the westward facing wall; glass being too much a concession to weakness, he had settled for sanding the walls as close to translucence as possible without physically excising the rock. The resulting illumination was both eerie and uncertain when contrasted with the butter-yellow light cast by a chandelier that hung so low it only accentuated the height of the room. The stone chair on the roughly-hewn dais at the end of the chamber cast an irregular set of layered shadows into the chamber's recesses.

Jared watched Noelle carefully as he led Geneviive

inside. Though the wolf-of-all-seasons did not slow, a twitch at the corner of her eye betrayed her unease.

Mariescha, Elijah, and Josephiat waited as requested near the center of the long hall, their shadows flickering around them in translucent pools. Jared reassured them with a smile as he drew near, then canted his ears forward smartly and summoned his official voice, several notes deeper than his usual low tenor.

"Gentlewoman, Goodmen, I bring you greetings."

Their response echoed softly in a major third. "My lord, my lady."

"This is not something often done," Jared said, "But today I would ask you to stand for a fealty ceremony again." He saw the question in their eyes and held out an open hand, indicating Noelle. "Geneviive and I have brought home to Dahrengard our long lost sibling, Noelle."

Of the three, only Elijah betrayed no sign of surprise—the outlands master had been privy to young Jared's plan to defy his father—but none of them asked. They were *sathet*—they knew what *pruschani* did to infants like Noelle.

"Noelle, these are the heads of the commonfolk of Dahrengard. Gentlewoman Mariescha is the mistress of the personal and grounds staff. Goodman Elijah is the outlands master, who cares not only for the beasts but speaks for those living far outside our walls. Goodman Josephiat is the inland master, and speaks for those within our walls and the immediate perimeter of the keep." Jared smiled again and said, "If you would prepare yourselves for the ceremony, please."

Geneviive walked behind them to the traditional position of witness as the three slowly descended to one knee and tilted their heads back. Noelle stared at them.

"Now what do I do?" she asked to Jared in a low voice.

"Clasp their throats with your hand," he answered. "Tell them you accept their rightful subordination."

Noelle's ears sagged. "You're jesting."

"I'm not. Haven't you ever seen our wild brothers? This is a modification of what they do for the Alpha pair. We thought," and here Jared paused to smirk, "that it was more dignified than forcing them to roll over and offer their bare midriffs."

Her cheeks proved easy to read without the soft pelt of most Hinichi. Noelle blushed as she walked to Mariescha. Heavy bones had given the woman an appearance of solidity despite the lack of any extra fat. Her graying hair had been tied back in a perfunctory braid, wisps escaping to frame a summer-colored face. Yellow eyes stared politely up at the chandelier. Hesitantly, Noelle placed the flat of her hand across Mariescha's throat. She let her fingers down one by one until they snugly clasped most of the woman's neck.

Clearing her throat, Noelle said, "I accept your . . . rightful . . . subordination. Gentlewoman."

"Amen," they murmured, and the wolf-of-all-seasons started. She snatched her palm away.

Geneviive said softly, "It's an informal ceremony, Noelle. You do well thus far."

Elijah's hands engulfed his knee entirely where they rested on his leg. Standing, the outland master would have loomed over Noelle, as if God had left him his tall, gangling frame as a relic of adolescence, forgetting to smooth it into the polish of an adult. Only the worn lines around his mouth and solemn brown eyes, and the heavy cords on the backs of his hands and his exposed neck spoke of age. Noelle lightly touched one of those sinews before covering it with her palm and folding her fingers down.

"I accept your rightful subordination, Goodman," she said quickly.

"Amen."

Noelle backed away, reminding Jared of a skittish *tolly*. He nodded once to her, and she approached Josephiat. The inland master had been built like a short battering ram: broad shoulders, bulging arms each the size of two of Geneviive's legs. His blackened fingertips in concert with his build told eloquent tales of his blacksmithing. He wore a God-braid down the right side of his face, where an old fight had claimed half of his ear.

"I accept your rightful subordination, Goodman," Noelle said as she covered his throat with her palm.

"Amen."

"Rise, all," Jared said. "And acknowledge your newest liege-lady."

"Lady," the three murmured, bowing to Noelle. Their voices layered over one another, pale echoes in the massive hall. "Welcome. Welcome-welcome. Welcome, Lady. Lady. Welcome Lady."

"Thank you," Noelle answered, tossing her head.

"You may return to the duties I interrupted so rudely," Jared said with a grin, winning back matching expressions. The three heads of household filtered into the corridors leading out of the audience chamber, leaving only Jared, Geneviive, and a wolf-of-all-seasons who fidgeted as much as her candlelit shadows.

"Would you like to see your rooms?" Geneviive asked. "There's time before Jared takes you out."

"Out?" Noelle glanced at him.

Jared folded his arms behind his back. "As second eldest, your duty within the triad is to speak for the people Dahrengard rules."

"I thought Goodman . . . Elijah? Did that."

Jared and Geneviive exchanged a look. Geneviive said, "Our father did not hold the same priorities we do. In the traditional way, one of the triad saw to the people who claimed Dahrengard as liege. He split those duties between Elijah and Josephiat instead. We would prefer to allow the goodmen to return to their original postings."

"Which were?"

"Master of stables and master of services."

Noelle looked from one to the other and said, "I see. So you are taking me to visit one of these. . . ."

"Villages, yes," Jared said.

"How long will it take?"

"Maybe three hours. We'll be heading for the Throat. It's beautiful in summer."

Noelle's particolored tail lashed once. "I'd rather just go, then."

Jared smiled. "Then go we shall."

While Noelle's awkward seat betrayed her inexperience at riding *tollies*, she'd listened to instructions on guiding them and then followed them rigorously on the trail. She adjusted rapidly enough to their rolling walk. The intermittent breeze tousled her soft white hair and stung color to her cheeks. She'd insisted on riding astride, like a man.

"So where exactly are we going?"

"To the Throat," Jared answered, rubbing the reins absently in his right hand as the trail unfolded. "It's the most prosperous area that tithes to Dahrengard."

Butterflies chased one another across the sturdy azure blossoms of the wild goodlips and terrapretties. Noelle's eyes tracked them. "Isn't it a little cold for butterflies?"

"It doesn't get much warmer than this here. Some number always manage to fly up far enough to see us. There'll be more of them in the Throat."

Noelle rolled her lip between her teeth, a mannerism that took Jared aback in its similarity to one of Geneviive's. He could sense her discomfort building, but ignored it to let her frame her questions. The path to the Throat from Dahrengard proper was one of the more beauteous ones, where the teeth of the mountain range lost their points, and then their girths, and then at last subsided into the gumless vista of an old man's mouth. Soft milk- and cream-colored flowers spread through the hoarfrost, breaking it into glassy slivers.

"Jared . . ."

His body tightened and he forced his ears to remain normal, canted forward. Such a soft voice, almost strangled by the emotions she'd been hiding from them.

"Yes?"

Her pause drew on too long. Jared knew when the question came that it would not be the one he'd been hoping for.

"Three hours. What's on the agenda afterwards?"

"Supper, and maybe a small dance and celebration."

Noelle's black-rimmed ears twisted, one flopping down and the other trying to turn completely off her head. Her obvious confusion would have been comic had it not been the marker of a greater tragedy. "A celebration?"

"Of course." Jared did not offer any more. She would have to come to the conclusion on her own.

"So tell me more about the . . . Throat. Is that the place in the tapestry?"

Jared glanced at her. "Yes, actually. The one in the entrance hall."

"With the herders," Noelle said carefully, meeting his gaze and then quickly looking away.

"Yes. The *birschot* herders. Good springy hair comes off the *birschot*. We make it into thread and dye it in the winter games."

Noelle wrinkled her delicate human nose, its underside just stiff enough to recall the thick nose-pad of a normal Hinichi. "Thread-dying is considered a game?"

Jared chuckled. "It's a festive time. We celebrate the colors of the seasons."

"Pardon?"

"The colors of the seasons," Jared said again, surprised. "You don't even know that, do you?"

"Maybe you hadn't noticed, but I didn't really grow

up properly."

The bitterness in her voice almost stopped his re-ply before Jared realized how important it was to keep from acknowledging it. "Hinichi come in definite color schemes, you would say. Winter colors are white and ivory. Autumn is black and gray. Summer runs to the deep browns and reds, while spring claims the yellow-ish browns and the oranges." He touched his own black cheek ruff. "You would call me an autumn-son with win-ter rising since I'm mostly black with these few patches of white on my face and my chest, while Geneviive is en-tirely summer's daughter in her shades and shadows of brown."

"What am I, then?" Noelle asked dryly. "A freak?"

Jared reined the *tolly* in as his unease caused it to side-step. Too close to the truth, if not the right reasons. "Hinichi like you are rare and your coloration is prized. You are called a wolf-of-all-seasons, and they say that there is more of the *Hinichisene* in you than in the rest of us. Born at all times at once."

"What is the *Hinichisene*?"

Jared sighed and then grinned. "Ask me where God is, and I might have a readier answer. It's . . . what it means to be one of us. The heart of things and people Hinichi. The fount from which our identity and heritage springs. Our history helped to make it, but it's more than that. It's something God puts in all of us."

"How mystical."

Jared frowned slightly. His sister rode with slumped shoulders, her eyes focused on a point just between the *tolly's* oveate ears. "The *Hinichisene* is in you, Noelle.

Stronger in you than in summer's daughter, or winter-rising autumn's son. You're one of the few wolves-of-all-seasons. Mark it well."

"I will," she murmured. "I only wonder who didn't."

"How did it go?" Geneviive whispered as Jared unpacked the wool sent by the village.

Jared's ears flipped back against his skull. "She can be difficult," he replied softly. "You never know when she's uncurling or if it's just your imaginings. And yet to see her . . . she has to touch everything, as if to make sure it's real." He shook his head. "Maybe you can do better with her than I have."

"Let me see," the smaller woman said, and then stepped away. "Noelle, come with me? I can take you to a nice bath before supper."

"I suppose it wouldn't be proper to be seen changing in mixed company," Noelle said, tail wafting to and fro.

Geneviive refused to blush. "Well, no," she replied.

Noelle chuckled. "Okay, then, 'sister'. I'm all for a bath."

"I know how it is. The rides are grueling. You think that because they're in the cold, you won't sweat, but somehow you do anyway." Geneviive smiled warmly at the taller woman and said, "It's this way." She slipped into a side corridor leading away from the audience chamber deeper and higher into the side of the mountain. Taking the fork on the right, she led her newfound sister into the small suite reserved for Dahrengard-*scain*.

"Nice living room," Noelle murmured, staring at the

oval-shaped nest with its rounded walls and the translucent rock windows. The hearth slept, lit only in the evenings in the summer. Thick rugs thrown on the stone floor alleviated the cold, and tapestries on the walls took the place of true windows save on the back wall where a massive viewscreen, flat and thin as any modern model displayed an image from the courtyard. "What's this?"

Geneviive grinned, ears pricking up and tail almost curling. "It's real-time," she said. "Grandfather wanted all the latest gadgets, but Father wasn't really . . . interested. He scuttled most of them. Jared and I want to bring them back, and then some. We're hoping to get u-bank connections as soon as we finish winter-stocking."

"A connection," Noelle whispered. "With the Alliance? What kind?"

"The whole thing. Real-time u-bank access, automatic updates, string-links to all the other services on the Core worlds, registration as a thread, genie data stream access and Well-pushed commlinks."

The wolf-of-all-seasons stared at her as if she'd grown wings. Geneviive actually felt her shoulders when the stare wound on too long. "Noelle? Did I say something wrong?" She pursed her lips. She'd studied the portfolio as avidly as Jared had when the courier had dropped it off.

"I . . . no. It would be a wonderful thing for Dahrengard."

Geneviive nodded. "We think so. But there'll be time enough for that kind of thing later. Won't you come bathe? We haven't assigned a maidservant to you yet, but I'll be glad to assist you."

"A maidservant?" Noelle's mezzoalto faltered up the scale into a squeak. "I don't need help to bathe."

"It's different from what you're accustomed to," Geneviive said. "We don't have automated showers. Someone has to wash your back and hair." She touched her own pale blonde braid.

"I suppose. . . ."

"Trust me," Geneviive said, smiling, and led the way up the small stairs set into the side of the chamber. She pushed the pocket door back, releasing a faint cloud of steam. "Be careful on these steps, they're slippery."

The steam thickened as she ascended, her ears reporting Noelle's footsteps behind her. The top of the stairs opened onto the smooth platform of a round chamber, the domed ceiling and its entire outward facing wall smoothed to milky translucence. The weak sun glowed, a brighter smudge against the very top of the chamber.

Noelle gasped, then cleared her throat and said, "I thought you told me it wasn't polite to change in mixed company . . . and now you want me to bathe in a gazebo?"

Geneviive laughed. "Oh, this is one of the top rooms in the keep . . . and even if you're in one of the needle-towers, you can't see through the stone on a clear day."

"I suppose it's like a privacy screen," Noelle said to herself, and chuckled. "Natural glass-frosting. It's nice."

A shallow, smooth oval had been cut into the flat floor, clear water bubbling in it and releasing the clouds of steam that had been beading on Geneviive's fur up the stairs. She shed her long skirts, bodice and over-tunic, leaving only her expensive floor-length cotton shift.

Noelle crouched beside the pool. "Do you pipe this all the way up from the hot springs? Ow! It's hot!"

Geneviive folded her arms under her breasts and waited.

The wolf-of-all-seasons laughed. "Okay. That was dumb."

Geneviive wondered if the blush was on account of the heat, or if Noelle was actually embarrassed. She was slow to peel off her boots. Her tunic and pants took even longer. Geneviive had almost decided to offer her aid when Noelle finally pulled off the last layer.

"Oh!"

Noelle froze, her shoulders curling inward.

Geneviive stepped closer, one hand outstretched. "Oh!" she said again, her throat round with wonder. "Noelle . . . Noelle, you're beautiful."

"W . . . what?"

She realized then that the hunched shoulders and folded ears were shame, not surprise. More firmly, she repeated, "You're beautiful. I didn't think . . . no fur! Almost anywhere. Smooth, like a human, but all the colors of the seasons, and . . . and a pattern to them. . . ."

Noelle stared at her, lower lip dragging down from upper. "I didn't think you were cruel."

Remembering Jared, Geneviive reached out and grabbed Noelle's shoulders, gazing directly into her eyes. "I am not lying, by God's word, I'm not!"

"You think I'm beautiful?" Noelle whispered.

"Yes!"

"Not . . . not abnormal? Not a mutant?"

Geneviive's stomach twisted at the hunger and

hopelessness in the twist of dark brows and hoarfrost eyes. "No!"

Noelle searched her face, and then shook Geneviive loose. She unfolded herself from her seat and stood . . . and pirouetted slowly, arms outstretched and tail lifted. A dark ridge of black ran down her spine to spill at her tail, and from this ridge other colors flowed, running over one another to wrap around her body like fragile petals. Geneviive remembered, briefly, her mother telling her how fine painters layered films of color one over the other to create a rich, textured surface complete with all the implied fragility of its building. Noelle reminded her of a painted flower, a living one.

Steam rose in arabesques around the wolf-of-all-seasons as she deliberately descended into the water, dispelling the magic of the moment.

Geneviive took a deep breath. She hunted for soap crystals and a stiff brush. "I wish I had your ears," she said wistfully, to break the silence.

"My ears?" Noelle asked, mystified. She stiffened when Geneviive reached over and poured water down her white mane, but her shoulders relaxed as the brush began to work through its knots.

"Oh yes. Great-grandmother had Mother Mary ears, but she didn't see fit to bequeath them to me!"

The tension yoking Noelle's shoulder blades together bled slowly away. The wolf-of-all-seasons chuckled. "Should I even ask."

"The opaque white-furred insides, the pale backs and the black rims . . . they're like the ears of the clan runt, Rebeka, that Mother Mary praised for her loveliness.

That's why we call them so. You'll have no end of suitors if you stay here, with such beguiling ears."

Noelle rolled one of the soap crystals between her fingers until it broke, studying the resulting powdery granules. "Somehow I've never thought of people's ears being 'beguiling'," she said, bemused.

Geneviive laughed, running the brush through the long white hair. "Well, you'll learn."

"Geneviive, what are the braids? Do they mean something?"

"The braids?" Geneviive paused. "You mean the ones tied with beads? Here, take some more of those crystals. A little more rubbing'll yield a nice lather. You're talking about the braids like Goodman Josephiat's."

Noelle nodded, pulling a knot into the brush with the movement. "I've seen other people wearing them. Especially in the village. Is it just a fad?"

Pleased and surprised at her sister's facile eyes, Geneviive fumbled with the knot, picking it out with her fingers. She slipped her feet into the hot water on either side of Noelle's ribcage. "Those are Godbraids. The lowlanders call them 'prayer-plaits'. You braid them when you want to remind yourself and God of one of your prayers to Him. If it's a petition, you braid them with faceted crystals. If it's to show gratitude, then you bead them with cabochons. And if you're just remembering someone in your prayers, you use metal beads, and sometimes little decorations that remind you of that person."

Noelle paused, one soap-sudded hand rubbing her forearm. "So what if you're thanking God for a petition he granted for your best friend?"

Geneviive laughed. "Gratitude always takes precedence over petitions, and petitions over people when you're deciding how to decorate them. And you always take out a separate braid for each prayer."

"You're not wearing one for your father."

Geneviive's hand fumbled, dropping the brush into the water. She reached down to fish it off the current. "Well. Father isn't exactly the kind to look down out of Heaven and notice."

"You didn't like him much, did you?"

"Children owe their parents obedience. The Good Book never said anything about love." Geneviive walked to the bench on the side of the chamber. "We'll have to put your clothes to the wash. I'll go get something for you to borrow in the mean-time."

Noelle twisted in the waters, her hands clasping the edges of the pool. "No skirts, please! Or dresses. They're so . . ." She stopped at Geneviive's lifted brow. "I'm not used to them," she finished, ears sagging.

"It's not proper for woman to be seen in men's clothing."

"I'm not a proper Hinichi," Noelle said. "Geneviive . . . even if I stay, I might never be a proper Hinichi. . . ."

"If?" Geneviive asked softly, then waved a hand. "Never mind, Noelle-sister. I'll get you some men's clothing . . . for now. We can discuss setting an example for the young ones later." She slipped into the stairwell before the wolf-of-all-seasons could reply, her lips pressed together in a hard line and the shape of her eyes reflecting her worry.

The scent of pricklelemon and fosfur seeds wafted from the kitchen into the dining hall. Preparations for supper neared completion, and the chaos in the hall might well have been choreographed, so flawlessly did the several score servants dance among the tables, setting places, hauling trays, flashes of colors earth-dark and winter-pale. Geneviive stood beside her brother, fussing with the thick wool of her purple skirts, her ears pinned to her head in her agitation.

"I just don't know, Jared. She's so hard to read. I think she's so near to us, though, so near. Just a little longer and we might get to her."

"I know it's evil to speak of the dead, but—"

"Jared . . . !"

"—But Father might as well have killed her, *decherna*! You know it's so. We might just be in time to save her."

"Jared!" Geneviive's eyes shone with startled tears. "How could you say such things?"

"What's an ugly truth spoken of the deceased when weighed against this reality?" Jared demanded in a low voice, ears sinking. "We should have all defied him. Me, Mother, the aunts and midwives who knew and didn't tell their husbands and children. Customs sometimes hurt people, Geneviive. Sometimes they kill people."

Geneviive covered her face. "Oh, Jared. I wish . . . I wish it had been different."

"Wishes and prayers, *decherna*," the Hinichi man said, sighing. "But at least, now, we have a chance. Where is she? They're already seating the old ones."

Geneviive scanned the crowd, separating the servants leading the thin-blooded Dahrengard elders to their seats, then stood on tip-toe. "There . . . by the entrance, looking bewildered. I'll fetch her. Noelle!" Waving, she pushed through the elaborate dance, cutting ragged holes in the rhythm. The wolf-of-all-seasons hugged herself in the shadow of the entrance, dressed in dark blue tunic and breeches of Hinichi cut. Her damp hair curled around her face where it didn't stick to her back.

As Geneviive approached, Noelle asked, "Is dinner always this big a commotion?"

"This is a commotion?" Geneviive asked, gently teasing. When the taller woman didn't smile, she said, "Yes, we always eat this way. The entire keep comes together, as God intends, to break our bread. Come sit with us."

Noelle followed, unresisting, allowing Geneviive to place her between herself and Jared. She sat with the others when the bells sounded, running her palms over the hard stone table.

Geneviive and Jared both tasted their supper with new palates, imagining they had never eaten in Dahrengard and glancing occasionally at their guest. The cooks had outdone themselves with the fowl, dressing and stuffing it with the fosfur's seeds and fibrous Saint's Foot herb, a tangy delicacy. The dry wine had a floral hint, just a touch of wood—imported from the lowlands in the shadows of the Teeth, where soil was less recalcitrant. By the time the aftersoups in their bread trenchers had been cleared from the table, Geneviive felt her confidence renewed. Noelle had eaten heartily, her reticence to rip at the food with her hands swiftly dissipating under the pressure of her tactile curiosity. She nursed the wine after the food vanished, fingers splayed across the lip of the heavy pewter goblet.

Goodman Elijah walked to the threshold before the table of the Dahrengard-*scain* and bowed, awaiting permission to speak. Jared glanced at Geneviive, who shrugged ever-so-slightly. He smiled, hiding his bewilderment.

"Goodman, pray you, tell us what brings you to our table?"

Elijah stretched his lanky frame upwards. "Master, me and mine want to toast the new one." He lifted his goblet in a bony hand, his action mimicked behind him by the servants standing respectfully at their tables. Elijah trained his eyes directly on Noelle and said, "We're glad to be having you back, milady. We'd be pleased if you would stay. You were missed."

Noelle's hands tightened on her cup. "Was I?" she managed, her voice a rasp.

"As it please the Lord, you were," Elijah confirmed. He lifted his cup and said, "To the young mistress."

"God's blessings." The benison rode up to the table like the summer wind.

Noelle stood, listing to one side. She twisted around and took one dignified step, then stumbled and ran from the hall. Jared and Geneviive sprang to their feet and pursued her, up corridors lit by sconces back to their rooms.

Noelle huddled by the fire on her knees, head bowed and hair spilling, white milk, against the flagstones of the hearth. Her shoulders leaped and shook, though she made no sound. Geneviive hastened to her side as Jared closed the portal.

"Noelle! Oh, Noelle, you're not. . . ."

The wolf-of-all-seasons lifted her face. Firlit trails streaked her cheeks and dark spots on the stone testified to the length of her tears.

"Noelle, *decherna*," Jared said, his voice low.

"Stop it!" she cried. "Stop calling me that! How can you call me that! I don't understand!"

"Don't understand what?" Geneviive asked, trying to reach out and touch one of the jerking shoulders.

Noelle tossed her head, hair whipping around her chest. "You call me 'sister!' You say I'm ruler over your people! You say I belong here, that I'm beautiful, that I'm special and God-touched and even your servants toast me! Well, if I'm so God-cursed special, why did you abandon me in the first place?"

Sparks popped in the ensuing silence.

Jared walked forward and crouched in front of Noelle. Her breasts heaved as she swallowed past her sobs, dark brows pulled inward, the blood-shot whites of her eyes darker than her hoarfrost blue irises. "I will unriddle you that, Noelle. But you must trust my answer, and that Geneviive and I are not here to harm you."

Geneviive gently unsealed Noelle's hands from the hearth, receiving only one wild look of agonized uncertainty. Shaking, Noelle bowed her head, then looked up at Jared from beneath a trembling, ragged fall of white hair.

"You know by now that our father did not always see our ways," Jared said, waiting until the wolf-of-all-seasons nodded. "He was a follower of what we call the *pruscha*. Grandfather, Mother, Dahrengard in general has always been of the *sathet* sect, but Father . . . no one could gainsay him. When he became Lord of the holding, the *pruscha* was the law, no matter what we thought."

"What does that have to do with me?" Noelle asked, still quivering, her face, her heart finally vulnerable.

"The *pruscha* is a stricter sect than the *sathet*," Jared said, willing her to feel his sincerity. "They believe that pride is the worst of the seven deadly sins. They preach that there once lived a group of Hinichi called the Berena that wanted to be as great as the messiah. They began to breed among each other purposefully to reach a point where they were made in his image. Not as the messiah had made them—wolf-like with thoughts and the shapes of men—but as the messiah was."

He tipped up her chin in his finger, aware of Geneviive's brilliant eyes immediately to his right. "Human, Noelle. They wanted to be human."

A new tear rolled down her cheek as Noelle's eyes thinned and she drew in a sudden breath.

Jared said, "The *pruschani* believe babes born too human in seeming are demons sent to tempt the Hinichi into doing as the Berena did. They leave those infants to die in the cold. That's what Father forced Mother to do to you."

The whine that whispered out of Noelle's throat had no match in Jared's memory. He had never heard such a sound. He prayed he never did again.

"Because . . . of my face?"

"And your skin," Geneviive murmured, saddened.

"How did I . . . I should be dead!"

"Jared went after you."

Noelle looked sharply at Jared, eyes widening. "You . . . ?"

"With Elijah's help," Jared said, letting one knee down to the floor and propping his free hand on the other. "I was newly seven years old, and Geneviive hadn't even been born. I found out from one of the midwives' children what had happened. Elijah advised me, but I told no one else what I planned. I followed the servants out to the hill and waited until they'd gone, then took you to the nexus of the Alliance embassy at the base of the Teeth. The doctor there promised me he would get you off-world, where you could have a chance to live."

"Then when Father died," Geneviive said, stroking Noelle's hand, "We sent for you right away. So you could come home."

"Why . . . why couldn't you. . . ."

"Father was not a reasonable man," Jared said, his voice gentle. "If we had defied him, he would have killed you himself. It was the only way we could think of to save you."

Noelle slumped against Geneviive. "It's so much. I need time."

"You have all the time in this world," Jared said. "Sleep, take the days at your pace. This is your home."

Noelle glanced up at him, then nodded swiftly and stared at her folded legs. The fire cast a halo across her glossy hair. She said nothing for several minutes, then repeated the word, as if it were new, as if it were curious and uncomfortable and wondrous.

"Home."

Noelle clasped each of them to her with all the strength in her lithe frame. Geneviive found herself surprised at the hunger in the embrace; returning it, she barely missed smashing her nose against a ladyshoop, the bloom faded but still faintly scented.

"I hate to think that I've disappointed you," the wolf-of-all-seasons was saying, the wind tousling the fur collar of her tunic. "I promise whatever I decide I'll come back myself and tell you. You've earned that much. It's just that . . ."

"You don't need to explain," Jared said, gripping her shoulder and squeezing affectionately. "You've been out there all your life. You need to think in the quietude of the places that are familiar."

"Just remember that we'll be here for you always, whatever you decide," said Geneviive fervently.

"I know," Noelle said, sounding surprised. She picked up her bag and said, "I'll send back word. Be well!"

Jared grinned. "We will. God touch your head!"

Noelle's smile grew shyly in return. She turned and trotted toward the sleek shuttle hunkered on the tarmac, her shadow stretching eastward across the dark pavement.

Geneviive leaned against Jared as he waved. She sighed, watching the figure recede. "Oh, Jared. She came with the summer and is leaving with it. I had so hoped she would stay."

"She'll be back," Jared said, so firmly that Geneviive

pulled away to look at his face. He was still grinning, his arm defining an arc in the air.

"How do you know?"

Jared only smiled. Geneviive turned her gaze toward the figure on the tarmac that was pausing at the shuttle's stairs to wave. Summer's waning sunlight glowed in the metal beads that marked the two braids tangled in white, white hair.

AFTERWORD

CREAKY ME WAS AROUND when the first Furry fans started gathering around Steve Gallacci at s-f conventions in 1980. Furry fandom slowly grew during the '80s. The first fanzine with amateur Furry fiction and art was Kyim Granger's *FurVersion*, twenty-one issues from May 1987 to November 1990.

Most "Furry small-press magazines" were very small and short-lived, but *Yarf!: The Journal of Applied Anthropomorphics* ran for sixty-nine issues from January 1990 to September 2003. One of the first things in the first issue was a drawing by Micah, then Maggie de Alarcon. The only information about her was that she was very young, and she lived in Florida.

Maggie had art regularly in *Yarf!* through 1998. In *Yarf!* #51, December 1997, she started using the nickname of Micah. She had her first short story, "Two Uniforms", in *Yarf!* #50, September 1997. This introduced us to Alysha Forrest and the universe of the Pelted. With "Cold and Gentle Dark" in *Yarf!* #52, April 1998, she was signing her stories as M. C. A. 'Micah' Hogarth. By then she was writing for other Furry small-press magazines besides *Yarf!*, notably *PawPrints Fanzine*. Two years later, she wrote all of her Alysha Forrest short stories together into a 157-page novel, *Alysha's Fall* (Cornwuff Press, September 2000).

Not all of her stories featured Alysha Forrest, but all were set in her Pelted universe. One of these was "Rosettes and Ribbons" in *Yarf!* #58, January 2000, which was selected for the first anthology of Furry "best" fiction, *Best in Show*, in July 2003. Another was "Butterfly" in *Anthrolations* #1, January 2000. The last Alysha Forrest to be published in a magazine was "In the Line of Duty" in *Anthrolations* #7, November 2003. It won the 2003 Ursa Major Award for Best Anthropomorphic Short Fiction of the year.

Shortly after that, almost all Furry small-press magazines had ceased publication, except those that featured Furry eroticism, for lack of submissions. Her short fiction appeared sparsely for a few years, until print-on-demand, and Smashwords and Kindle publishing made it practical for her to publish her own books and short stories, the latter as Kindle booklets. She had already begun to create other universes besides the Pelted: there have been the Jokka series, introduced in "Money for Sorrow, Made Joy" in the online weekly *Strange Horizons*, 26 November 2001; the Kherishdar series, introduced in the "chapbook" *The Aphorisms of Kherishdar* (CreateSpace, March 2008); and the Spots the Space Marine series, begun as a web serial from February 2009 to June 2011 and published with sequels on Kindle since then. Today there are Jokka and Kherishdar novels as well as short fiction, published under CreateSpace and Hogarth's imprint of Stardancer Studios, and standalone novels such as *Flight of the Godkin Griffin* (Sofawolf Press, June 2012).

Hogarth was briefly involved in a controversy in January 2013 when Amazon.com removed the Kindle edition of *Spots the Space Marine* from its sales, in response to a complaint from a U.K. games developer, Games Workshop, that her book had violated its trademark on the phrase "space marine" in its game *Warhammer 40,000: Space Marine*. Hogarth reported this online, and soon dozens of outraged bloggers pointed out that "space marine" has been a generic term in science fiction since the 1930s, used by authors as prestigious as Robert A. Heinlein. Hogarth got numerous supporters, including some well-known s-f personalities and the Electronic Frontier Foundation, which editorialized that Games Workshop was a "trademark bully". A month later, *Spots the Space Marine* was back on Amazon.com.

She is the creator of successful Kickstarter campaigns. Aside from all of the above, she remains a private person in the Furry world. Her online biography is: "Daughter of two Cuban political exiles, M.C.A. Hogarth was born a foreigner in the American melting pot and has had a fascination for the gaps in cultures and the bridges that span them ever since. She has been many things—web database architect, product manager, technical writer and massage therapist—but is currently a full-time parent, artist, writer and anthropologist to aliens, both human and otherwise."

Her fiction has variously been recommended for a

Nebula, a finalist for the Spectrum, placed on the secondary Tiptree reading list and chosen for two best-of anthologies; her art has appeared in RPGs, magazines and on book covers."

Claws and Starships contains six Pelted stories that do not feature Alysha Forrest. Hogarth – Maggie – has asked me to write this foreword and afterword because I have been an enthusiastic fan of her art and writing for over two decades, and I have just edited a Furry anthology, *What Happens Next* (FurPlanet Productions, July 2013) with one of her newest Pelted stories in it. I am honored to be in one of her books at last, instead of just reading or reviewing it.

—Fred Patten

ABOUT THE AUTHOR

M.C.A. HOGARTH HAS been many things—a web database architect, product manager, technical writer and massage therapist—but is currently a parent, artist, writer and anthropologist to aliens. She has over forty titles available in the genres of science fiction, fantasy, humor and romance.

Twitter: twitter.com/mcahogarth
Website: mcahogarth.org

CPSIA information can be obtained
at www.ICGtesting.com
Printed in the USA
BVHW092157140122
626346BV00013B/583